The Fox of Skelland

By the same author

Black Nest

The
Fox of Skelland

by

Rachel Dixon

Illustrated by Neil Reed

VIKING KESTREL

VIKING KESTREL

Published by the Penguin Group
27 Wrights Lane, London W8 5TZ, England
Viking Penguin Inc., 40 West 23rd Street, New York, New York 10010,
USA
Penguin Books Australia Ltd, Ringwood, Victoria, Australia
Penguin Books Canada Ltd, 2801 John Street, Markham, Ontario,
Canada L3R 1B4
Penguin Books (NZ) Ltd, 182–190 Wairau Road, Auckland 10, New
Zealand

Penguin Books Ltd, Registered Offices: Harmondsworth, Middlesex,
England

First published 1989
10 9 8 7 6 5 4 3 2 1

Filmset in (Linotron 202) Palatino by
Rowland Phototypesetting Limited (London) Ltd

Printed in Great Britain by
BPCC Hazell Books Ltd
Member of BPCC Ltd
Aylesbury, Bucks, England

A CIP catalogue record for this book is available from the British Library

ISBN 0–670–82612–X

For my parents

Chapter One

I thought nothing interesting would ever happen again when my best friend Emma left Skelland. I spent the morning after she left sitting on the fence opposite The Fox and Lady, watching the new people move in and hating it as much as I had hated seeing Emma's family moving out the day before.

The removal van arrived first. It was shiny yellow. On its side were the words:

SMOOTH MOVE the ones to trust

A denim-trousered youth leapt out of the cab.

'Mornin' darling,' he called, flicking back his greasy hair. 'You gonna give us a hand then?'

I scowled at him.

An older man climbed out of the other side. He looked like my Uncle Bob.

'Cat got your tongue?' said the youth.

'Leave her alone, Gary,' said the other man. 'Her mother's probably told her not to talk to strangers, and they don't come much stranger than you.'

He winked at me. I tried to smile, but it came out crooked. It's not easy to smile when your insides are churned up.

Their furniture was nothing special, but I've never found piles of mattresses or the backs of people's wardrobes very interesting.

Dean and Nick Kilby glided into the pub car park on their BMX bikes and did fancy manoeuvres over a bit of corrugated iron. Idiots. I hoped they'd get punctures. They were twins but, although they were identically irritating, they were easy to tell apart. They lived next door to me and always played their stereo full blast when I was trying to do my homework. When they saw me watching them they raced over and screeched to a dramatic halt just by my knees. I managed not to flinch.

'Having a good time Samantha?' said Nick. He knew I preferred to be called Sam. 'Like to snoop into other people's business do you?'

'Yeah,' said Dean. 'Seen anything interesting? Got any valuables have they?'

'You wouldn't *believe* what I've just seen going in there,' I said, trying to sound conspiratorial.

They looked interested.

'Tell us,' said Nick.

'They might hear,' I whispered.

They drew in closer.

'Tell,' said Dean aggressively.

'A *chair*,' I said.

They were not amused, but it was worth the pinched elbow and tugged hair.

'Cretins,' I shouted, when they were out of earshot.

Half a dozen tea chests later a car pulled up. It was a battered brown estate and seemed to be full of pot plants, like a botanical garden on wheels. A woman climbed out of the driving seat. Her trousers were crumpled and she looked harassed.

The youth staggered down from the removal van, trying to look busy under a pile of duvets.

'Hello darlin',' he said to the woman. 'Good drive?'

'No,' she said irritably. 'And it's Mrs Goddard to you.'

She leaned into the car and said, 'Get out, you two, and don't break any more leaves off the cheese plant.'

I was half expecting to see a couple of yucca plants sidling obediently past her, but instead two children squeezed their way out, a boy first, then a girl. The boy was a year or two older than me and obviously fancied himself. It looked as though he had done his hair with gunge and his clothes coordinated, even his socks. The girl was worse, a skinny shrimp of a kid with thin short hair sticking out all over her head. She wore an outsized sweatshirt that stopped at her knees and sloppy black shoes. I was *not* impressed.

Uncle Bob Lookalike came out.

'You made it then?' he said pleasantly to their mother. 'You look as though you could do with a cup of tea. I've just taken in the kitchen boxes. Would you like me to search out the kettle for you?'

'Oh please,' she said gratefully. 'It's in the box with tea towels on top. I feel as if I've been driving for days.'

'Let's look at our rooms,' said the boy to his sister.

They ran into the pub, jostling each other.

'Your husband not with you then?'

'No. He promised to show the new landlord round The Parrot and Silver again before he left. He's got to get the train down this afternoon. I wish he was here. I don't think I can face all this alone.'

'Things'll look better after a cup of tea,' he said.

Things certainly didn't look better for me. I walked down Lady Lane towards the river. Three posh houses were being built in one of the fields. The contractors had hacked away the hedge to make the site entrance and tyre tracks of sticky yellow mud curved out of the gap in the direction of the village. Big lorries had pushed their way backwards and forwards between the remaining hedges and made them dusty with fumes. They had ruined the lane. Why couldn't people leave things as they were? I walked over the tracks and kicked a hefty clod of mud. It spun into the air and landed with a satisfying splat.

'Watch who you're kicking things at,' said a voice behind me.

It was Joseph Jenkins. He was on his way home. Once you got past the pub and the new development there were no buildings down the lane apart from Joseph's cottage. It was right next to the churned-up field.

'It wasn't meant for you,' I said.

He walked along beside me, his big black boots thudding on the lane. His steps were sprightly for a man of his age and though his clothes were old they were always neat. He wore dark brown trousers, a hand-knitted sweater of the same grey as his hair and a comfortable tweedy jacket with patched-up cuffs. On his head was a flat cap.

'Missing your pal, are you?' he said.

'It's not fair,' I said. 'Nothing will ever be the same again.'

'Time can't stand still, Sam,' he said kindly. 'Let's hope summat good'll come out of it. Come home with me and I'll find you a nice fresh egg for your tea.'

We heard enthusiastic yapping from down the lane. Barker, his little dog, had heard him coming and raced towards us with his stumpy paws barely touching the ground.

'Why wasn't he with you?' I said. 'I thought he never left your side.'

'He's a private sort of a dog is Barker,' said Joseph. 'He needs time to himself sometimes and I don't question it.'

He bent down to give the dog an affectionate scratch under the ears.

'He's covered with mud,' I said. 'He must have been nosing about the building site.'

'He doesn't nose, doesn't Barker,' said Joseph. 'He investigates.'

'He must be a private investigator,' I said.

Joseph grinned. The wrinkles at the corners of his eyes folded up like fans.

'I know some folks think I take Barker too seriously, but he's in a class of his own, he is.'

'His tricks are brilliant,' I said. 'Do you think the new people will let him do them in The Fox and Lady?'

'That I don't know,' he said gravely. 'I shall accept what comes, but I don't mind saying it'll be a bit of a blow to Barker if he can't perform. A dog needs a sense of achievement.'

Joseph's cottage was semi-detached. The adjoining cottage was derelict, with its doors and windows boarded up. Slogans had been daubed on its red brick walls with white paint and broken roof slates lay amongst the tangled weeds around it. The front gate had been wrenched off and fence posts stolen for bonfires.

Though in considerably better condition, Joseph's cottage was far from smart. There was a tiny garden at the front with a square of grass and weed and a couple of sad-looking hydrangea bushes. A concrete path led down the side of the house to a small back garden where thin chickens pecked dolefully around on rough ground.

It was the inside of his cottage that I loved. We always went in through the kitchen. This was primitive with an old stone sink and no hot water tap. There was electricity though and Joseph could heat his water on a second-hand Baby Belling. There was an inside loo but no bathroom. I always wondered how he managed to have a bath, but didn't like to ask. The living room fascinated me. The walls were papered with rose-covered wallpaper. It was hideous, but he hadn't the heart to change it because his wife Ruby had chosen it. Over it hung patterned plates with pictures of dogs and horses on them, funny old leather bags, binoculars, mirrors and a set of flying ducks. Joseph was a real collector. There was also a bookshelf full of old books and a sideboard covered with ancient lamps and jugs, all lovingly polished and dusted. There was just enough space for a big armchair, a table and two dining chairs with tapestry seats. A low stool was also pushed under the table. The front door, which led into this room, was permanently locked and curtained.

Narrow stairs went up from the living room to Joseph's bedroom. Also upstairs was his hobby room. Now he had retired from his job on the Cumbermouth railway he spent hours in there reading, listening to his radio, mending old lamps or sorting through his collection of postcards. He sometimes brought down a rare book or interesting old toy to show me, but the room itself was strictly private.

'Sit you down, lass,' said Joseph when we got inside. 'Let me brew up and we'll have a nice cuppa. We've plenty of time to find you an egg. Hens never hurry, so why should we?'

He came out with statements like that from time to time. I sat up at the table. I didn't like to go in his armchair because it was always covered with dog hairs, and anyway Barker had got there first. Joseph brought in the biscuit barrel.

'Ginger nuts,' he said. 'My Ruby was partial to them, you know, God rest her soul.' He squeezed into the armchair beside Barker. 'I saw the van outside the pub,' he said. 'D'you reckon the newcomers have got any kids?'

'Two,' I said. 'I've seen them. They look awful.'

'You shouldn't judge by appearances,' he said. 'Give them a chance.'

'The boy had *stuff* on his hair,' I said.

'It's what's inside his head that counts,' said Joseph.

I pulled a face. The kettle began to wheeze in the kitchen.

'I'll just brew up,' said Joseph.

He brought the tea in one of his weird tea pots. It was like the head of a schoolboy wearing a cap and the boy's long nose was the spout.

I couldn't think of much to say, so I helped myself to a biscuit and gulped some tea before it was cool enough. I looked at the picture of Ruby on the wall. It was a faded old photograph of her as a young woman. She had been so beautiful.

The clock cleared its throat and chimed huskily.

'Time I got The Foxer out,' he said. 'It's the first of September, Foxing month.'

He slid open the sideboard drawer and pulled out a framed photograph. It showed a large imposing figure dancing in swirling black robes. There was obviously someone beneath those robes, covered from the head downwards so that his face could not be seen. Sitting on his head was a tall pointed hat, and set in its side, orange against black, was the leering face of a fox.

Joseph dusted it with his cuff and propped it up against an old railway lamp.

'Some say he's sinister,' he said, 'but he keeps the evil away.'

I shivered. I had never liked the picture.

'Can we go and find an egg now?' I said.

Joseph gave me a sharp look.

'Aye, lass. We'll find an egg.'

I was glad to get outside. The hens clucked hopefully around Joseph's feet. He put his hand in his pocket and threw down a handful of seed then bent down and pulled an egg from under the bushes beside the dilapidated hen coop. A downy feather was stuck to it.

'I wonder if the Codlings remembered to tell the new people about Foxing Day,' I said. 'What if they throw the costume out by mistake?'

Joseph wiped the egg on his pullover and handed it to me.

'If they do that,' he said grimly, 'there'll be trouble.'

Chapter Two

That happened on the Friday.

By Sunday afternoon I was thoroughly fed up. It had rained for two days and the new term started tomorrow. I'd have to go back without Emma and, on top of that, my school skirt was the wrong length and had an indelible gravy stain right down the front. Mum was totally unsympathetic. She said she'd paid good money for the skirt and was not about to buy another one just because it was the wrong style. As for the gravy stain, she said it was my own fault for slopping food down my clothes and she wished some of the washing powder manufacturers would come and do their trials in *her* house.

To cap it all, I hadn't finished one of my holiday assignments. I'd meant to copy it up after Emma left. I thought it would fill the time, but when it came to it I'd spent most of the weekend lying on my bed, listening to tapes. What was happening to me? I'd never handed work in late before, apart from the time I was away with chickenpox. It was for Mrs Dean too. She *never* gave extensions.

The weather had dried up after tea, so I went for a walk. I lived in Elm Street, the main street in Skelland. I walked to the end, where it curved into Lady Lane. Things looked much the same at The Fox and Lady. I was glad. I liked it just the way it was. It wasn't open but I walked close to the door in the hope of catching some snippets of conversation. A warm beery smell wafted out of an open window, but I couldn't hear anything. I looked up at the sign. It was faded like an old oil painting and showed a mysterious lady, cloaked in white. It was impossible to see her face beneath her hood. She cradled a sharp-nosed fox in her arms and her slim hands were pale against the orange fur. On each long finger she wore an ornate ring.

I walked down to the building site. I had decided it was time I had a look round and had put my wellies on for protection. I would investigate the house furthest from the road where there would be less chance of being disturbed. I squelched past the first two houses and climbed a pile of breeze blocks. It was as I did my Olympic gymnastics along a wooden plank that I had the feeling I was being watched. The house was huge and detached with big black holes where the windows were going to be. I squinted up at the black caverns but nothing moved. Anyway, I wasn't doing anything wrong. I was just walking through a field the way I had a hundred times before. It wasn't my fault if someone had built some houses in it.

My boots were heavy with mud and sand so I scraped them on the step before going in through the front door hole. There was a strong smell of wood and cement inside. For a moment I thought I heard a rustling noise but it was probably just an old cement bag blowing about.

There wasn't much to see inside the house. I looked out of the front window to see what sort of a view they would get. Apart from the other houses, which were well set back, there was a clear view across acres of flat fields to Cumbermouth. The tower blocks and dockland cranes didn't look so bad from a distance. Over to the right, past Joseph's cottage, was the River Finn, recognizable only by its dykes. Beyond it was the village of Thorncoates.

I clumped through two huge rooms to a back window. I could hear a creaking noise upstairs but I wasn't scared. New houses probably creaked until their bits had settled into place. There it was again. I tried to whistle nonchalantly but it came out as a rather rude noise. It wouldn't hurt to look upstairs. That way I could be sure there was nobody about.

I walked into the hall.

'If there's anybody there, come out,' I said. 'You don't scare me.'

I felt rather foolish. I hadn't meant to say anything at all but the curve in the stairs made it impossible to see to the top.

Creak, creak, creak ... I heard footsteps slowly coming down the stairs.

17

'Hi, Sam,' said a voice.

Who was it?

The girl from The Fox and Lady slopped round the curve. She was wearing the same voluminous sweatshirt and silly shoes.

'I thought I'd bump into you eventually,' she said.

'Who said you could call me Sam?' I said rudely.

'It's your name, isn't it?'

'How do you know?'

'The Kilby twins told me. I asked them the name of the girl sitting on the fence on the day we moved in.'

'There's no law against sitting on a fence,' I said.

'I didn't say there was,' she said. 'Come up and look at the view at the back. You have to be careful in the bedrooms though. They haven't put all the floor-boards down yet.'

What a nerve. She talked about the view as if she owned it. I knew every inch of those fields, and she'd only lived in the place for a few days.

I followed her upstairs but didn't go over to the window straight away. She gazed out in silence. The fresh September air rushed in and made the cobwebs billow. I knew the view well. You could see over to Holme woods. There wasn't a path over the fields but you could easily get over to Holme Burton if you didn't mind climbing over a few fences. Most people took the winding road out of Skelland to get there but that took ages. Not that there was much to see when you got there, just the site of Holme Abbey, a few posh houses and Holme Burton Farm. Even that would change soon. The farmer had sold off a bit of land for development and I'd seen men with theodolites there at the end of term.

I walked over and stood beside the girl. She was a good deal shorter than me. I wondered how old she was.

When I looked out the view was different. Straight fences about twenty metres apart ran across the fields from beside the woods towards our site. Between them, like a scar, lay an ugly trench.

'They're building some more of these monstrosities over there,' said the girl.

Big words. She wasn't stupid.

'See the heap of yellow sausages near the Holme wood,' she said. 'They're gas pipes to connect the two new developments. They're about to lay them alongside the trench at that end.'

I was horrified.

'Don't worry. They'll tidy the fields up afterwards,' she said.

How did this girl know so much? She was beginning to annoy me.

'It makes me sick,' I said. 'And you make me sick. I'm going home.'

She seemed not to notice my anger.

'I'll probably see you on the bus tomorrow,' she said. 'I'm going to Stansholme School, same as you.'

Her friendly tone made me feel guilty. I didn't know why. She was probably the most irritating person I had ever met.

'What's your name anyway?' I said gruffly.

'Rib,' she said.

How ridiculous. I wished I hadn't asked.

Chapter Three

The journey to school was tedious. The bus called at Thorncoates, Newmansey, Holme Burton and Skelland to collect pupils for Stansholme Middle and Upper School. It was usually late and all the Skelland children had to wait on the corner of Elm Street and Cumbermouth Road, by the telephone box, whatever the weather. The trick was to get there early, then at least you got to sit on the bench. Some idiot had ripped most of the panels off, but if you were first you could sit at the end which had both seat and back. When it rained three or four of us could squeeze into the telephone box, but the smell was awful. It was probably better to get wet.

The usual crowd was there on the first day of term. Dean and Nick Kilby were squashed up at the good end of the bench while Sharlene (their older sister) was draped against the telephone box chewing gum and looking lovesick. There were several children from Rowan Street (it was at the other end of the village and I didn't know them very well), Cherinea Johnson from Beech Crescent, and Jayne and Baz Baldwin who lived opposite me.

'Morning Samantha,' said Nick. 'Give us a look at your G.S. assignment. I need to put a few finishing touches to mine.'

'Finishing touches!' scoffed Dean. 'He's only written the title and he couldn't spell that.'

'And how much have you done?' said Nick, pushing his twin off the bench.

'Nothing,' said Nick, sprawling on the dirty pavement. 'But at least I've got a good excuse.'

'Oh yeah?' said Dean.

'Yeah. Mental stress at having to live with you.'

They fought, rolling across the pavement and into the road. Nobody took any notice. They were always doing it.

'Here come the new kids,' said Cherinea. 'Anybody know what they're called?'

The twins stopped fighting.

'Yeah,' said Nick, trying to get the tear in the knee of his trousers to bind together again.

'Goddard,' said Dean rubbing his ankle. 'He's Jason and she's Kneecap or something.'

'It's Rib,' said Nick. 'She looks spare.'

'Look at his socks,' said Cherinea. 'Who does he think he is?'

They were maroon, to match his school tie. Sharlene looked interested for a second. It was probably the most effort she would put into anything all day.

The two newcomers marched up to the group as if they'd lived in Skelland for years. They might at least have had the decency to look nervous or something. Luckily the bus pulled up, so I didn't have to talk.

I sat on my usual seat, the second one back on the left, but it wasn't the same without Emma. Rib and Jason sat on the opposite seat, but I didn't look at them. Marlene, the bus driver, turned back before she drove off.

'Your mate gone then love? Never mind; life goes on.'

We arrived at Stansholme Middle later than I had hoped. It was important to get in early on the first day of term if you were to stand any chance of getting a coatpeg or a decent desk. As I jostled my way along to Year Three, the registration bell went. I wished I wasn't there. I should have had the foresight to develop a stomach bug overnight.

The school had an aura of cleanliness about it, more in the form of polish and disinfectant smells than anything you could see. The floors had probably been polished but they were already dusty with footprints. The paintwork was still as blistered and battered as ever. I cut through the school canteen where polish smells were overpowered by the stench of onions and minced beef from the kitchen. Pans clattered in there and the ladies sang cheerfully along with Radio Cumber.

The girls' cloakroom was at the far end of the third year corridor. Once there I searched amongst bulging P.E. bags and bulky coats for a peg. One was free, but was hanging so loosely by its only screw that it swung round and tipped my jacket on to the floor. Someone sniggered. A face peered round the loo door. It was Isabelle Podd, a detestable girl in my form who had obviously rigged the peg to catch unsuspecting idiots like me.

'Three down,' she said gleefully. 'Had a good holiday, Hinch?'

I stuck out my tongue. Babyish I know, but it *was* an emergency.

'Three down? *Rubbish*,' said a voice.

It was Rib.

She took her scissors from her school bag and used them as a makeshift screwdriver to tighten up the offending screw.

'That'll do for now,' she said. She gave Isabelle a smile of such acidity that it nearly peeled the paint off the loo door. Isabelle sidled sulkily into the Year Base.

'Mind if I hang my coat on the bottom bit?' said Rib. 'There aren't any more free pegs. I'm going to be in the same form as you, by the way.'

She hung up her coat and followed me into the form room. The noise was dreadful. Nick and Dean were scribbling in their G.S. books, having persuaded a boy to lend them his work, but everyone else was catching up on holiday news. I didn't want anything to do with it. Rib and I went to the only spare table. To my surprise it was quite unobtrusive, yet had a good view of the board. We soon discovered why it was free. One leg was shorter than the others. The trays for our books were no better. One was full of dried ink and rude words and the other had several nuggets of fossilized chewing gum stuck in the corner.

During registration we all copied our timetable from the board, the secretary dealt with lunch money and we went table by table to choose a library book. The familiar activities made me feel calmer. It was only when Miss Stark began to tell us a little about the work we would be doing over the next few weeks that I began to feel uneasy again. It all sounded so different. I was quite sure I would not be able to keep up. I wished Emma was there. She had always given me confidence. We handed in our G.S. assignments and then Science for Mrs Dean. It was when Miss Stark began to count them that my head started to feel tight. Waves lurched up and down in my stomach and the fluorescent lights seemed to flicker more vigorously. It was panic.

'We seem to be three short for Mrs Dean,' she said. 'Alan Bishop is absent, that counts for one, Rebecca Goddard is new, that's another . . .'

I put up my hand.

'Yes?'

'I'm afraid mine isn't quite finished,' I said.

'And your name?'

'Sam Hinch.'

'Samantha Hinch.'

She bundled up the pile of work.

'I suggest you take these books to Mrs Dean and explain to *her* why your work is not ready. I expect you have a good reason. She will be in her study.'

Isabelle turned round and smirked hideously.

Mrs Dean was the Deputy Head, but also taught some science. Her study was next to the staff room. The door was closed. I knocked.

'Come.'

I went in. She was consulting a huge timetable on the wall.

'I've brought the assignments from Miss Stark.'

'Thank you, Samantha. Put them on my desk please. All present and correct I trust?'

'There's a new girl,' I said, 'and Alan Bishop is away . . . and . . .'

'Yes?'

'And I'm afraid I haven't done mine.'

'The reason?'

She didn't raise her voice, but there was a slight edge to it. I shrugged. It was about the worst thing I could have done.

'I'm afraid, young lady, that a shrug is *not* an acceptable excuse,' she said. 'I expect something more than that from one of my better pupils.'

Then I did something even worse. I cried. Not just a snivel either. It came in huge sobs that took me so much by surprise that they made my chest ache. I wept for the fact that I'd not done my work and spoiled my good record, and with nervousness about school, but most of all I wept for the loss of Emma. I hadn't cried about it before, not even on the day she left.

And then I felt an arm around my shoulders and a scented hanky pressed into my hands.

'That's right, dear,' said Mrs Dean. 'You have a good cry. That's a cry that needed to come out. Sit yourself down for a moment until you feel a bit better and then we'll see if we can come to some agreement about the assignment. It's not as though you've let me down before. There's no hope of me having time to mark them until the weekend anyway. The timetable's *right* up the creek.'

'I'm sorry,' I said. 'About my work. I did *mean* to do it.'

'Am I allowed to know what went wrong?' she said, pushing me into a low seat. She sat on the edge of her desk and waited.

'*Everything*'s gone wrong,' I said, tugging at the lacy corner of her hanky.

'It's not something to do with your friend leaving, is it? she said.

I must have looked surprised. You don't expect teachers to notice things like that. I nodded.

'I've done all the notes,' I said. 'I was going to write it all up after Emma had gone . . . to fill the time . . . but I couldn't seem to settle to it. We used to sit and do our work together sometimes, not to copy, but just to keep each other company . . . and . . .'

'So,' she said, 'you're low . . . and a bit lonely. That's bound to happen when you lose something that's important to you. Have you written to Emma yet?'

I shook my head.

'Well, I suggest you do that. Tell her how you feel and what you've been doing. She's probably having a far worse time at school than you are. She won't know *anybody*. And when you've poured out your heart to her, see about writing up some of my assignment. How would a week do?'

It was unbelievably generous. I managed a smile.

'I'll bring it next Monday,' I said. 'For definite.'

'Good,' she said. 'Off you go. Miss Stark will be wondering what I've done with you.' Her voice was brisk. She turned to the timetable again.

As I was about to shut the door she called after me.

'And Samantha,' she said. 'You can return the hanky then as well.'

I didn't really want to go back into the classroom. My face would be blobby from crying and they'd all know. Luckily Miss Stark was giving out heaps of new exercise books, so nobody noticed me coming in.

'OK?' whispered Rib.

Her sympathetic tone of voice made me feel like crying again. I nodded.

'Mrs Dean's all right really,' I said. 'I'll tell you about it at break.'

'I don't think much of these Maths exercise books,' said Rib. 'The staple's come out of mine already.'

For a moment she sounded like Emma.

We walked down to the far end of the field at break. I told Rib about my encounter with Mrs Dean, but I missed out the bit about crying. Rib didn't look like the sort of person who cried. The grass was still quite dewy under the trees at the edge of the field and it made our socks wet. A blackbird eyed us from a pyracantha bush. It pecked up a berry and held it in the end of its beak, like a pea in a pod, before swallowing it.

'What do you make of Stansholme Middle then?' I said.

'It's all right I suppose. It's my third change of school and they all seem pretty much the same to me. Miss Stark seems OK, doesn't she?'

'Yes.'

I couldn't think of much else to say so I asked her about their new house.

'Have you got your room sorted out yet?'

'Yes, but it's not the one I wanted. Jason got the one with the view over to Cumbermouth.'

'That was my friend Emma's room,' I said.

'She was lucky,' said Rib. 'All I've got is a view over the car park at the side.'

'Poor you,' I said. 'What did you do this weekend, apart from going to the building site?'

'Chores mainly. Mum and Dad believe in everyone lending a hand. We had to clear out the outhouses and garden shed. Your friend's parents had left stuff in them. They'd asked some chap in the village to clear it out but he got bronchitis. They hadn't got time to deal with it so they left Mum some money for a skip. It's been a real nuisance. *I* got the coal house to do. What a tip. It was full of absolute junk: old tyres, a watering can with a hole in it and even the skeleton of an old

27

Christmas tree. As if that wasn't enough, I had to get rid of two spiders, big ones with fat bodies and hairy legs. Jason got the cushy job as usual. He was clearing out the brick shed. There was a light in there and not a tarantula in sight.'

She paused for breath, but not for long.

'Shall I tell you the trick Jason played on me?'

I nodded.

'He carried a wooden box round to the skip. He'd found it in the shed. It said FOX on the top. "Look in here," he said, as if he'd found the Crown Jewels.

'I nearly died when I opened it. I pulled out a load of black material, a bit like curtains, and underneath it was a fox's head. I'm not joking. It was stuffed, like the ones people stick on their walls, but it didn't half stare at me. Ugh! The oddest thing was that it was set in the side of a huge black witch's hat. I didn't fancy touching it so I threw it into the skip with a shovel.'

They'd thrown the costume away.

'When are they moving the skip?' I said.

'That's just what *I* wanted to know. Mum said it should be collected this afternoon, but you know what these people are like. We'll probably have a bit of dead fox in our car park for days!'

I hoped she was right. I had an uneasy feeling in my stomach. I'd watched the Foxing ceremony every year for as long as I could remember. Most people did not believe all the superstitions surrounding it, but one or two of the older villagers would be very upset if anything went wrong. Den Critchley certainly wouldn't like it, not that I cared about *him*. He was chairman of the Skelland Life Committee and very bossy. It was Joseph that I was concerned about. He felt very strongly that if anything happened to affect the Foxing Day ceremony there would be trouble. I really didn't want to see him upset. I'd have to get home in time to do something about it.

I decided to say nothing to Rib. I didn't want her to think I believed in all that nonsense.

Chapter Four

The bus journey home took far longer than usual. There were road works on Skelland Road and even when Marlene had got past them she seemed to be in no hurry. The bus crawled along.

Rib was a problem too. She sat next to me and talked about school. I wondered if I ought to invite myself round to the pub when we got home, but even if the skip was still outside, I could hardly leap into it and start rummaging about in their rubbish. Joseph was the one to talk to. I decided to go straight to his cottage. I could see if the skip was still there on the way.

When we got back to Skelland I said goodbye to Rib, went home to let Mum know I was back, then walked down Lady Lane. To my relief, the skip was in the pub car park, but instead of going straight to Joseph's as I had planned I found myself walking over to it. I don't know what made me do it. I looked around to see if anyone was watching and peered into the skip.

The Fox was near the top. He was horrible. His yellow teeth leered out from amongst broken bottles and faded newspapers and his glassy eyes were almost alive. I turned and ran. I wanted to get away as quickly as possible. It was only when I was safely out on Lady Lane that I looked back. It was probably my imagination, but I thought I saw an upstairs curtain twitch.

My heart sank when I reached Joseph's cottage. A battered old van was parked outside. Its back doors were tied together with a length of fraying string and its rusty blue paintwork was covered in grime and blobbed with mud. It belonged to Nora and Sid Hambly. Although they were pleasant enough, I wished they weren't there. I needed to see Joseph alone.

'Come in Sam,' said Joseph.

The kettle whistled shrilly on the Baby Belling.

'You're just in time for a cuppa.'

He warmed a tea pot shaped like a rocking horse and popped in three tea bags.

'Guess who's here,' he said.

'Nora and Sid,' I said, trying not to sound too glum. 'I do need to have a word with you.'

'Of course, dear. You carry in the biscuit barrel and we'll all have a chat together.'

He poured boiling water over the tea bags, making them splutter, and stirred them around with a fork handle.

We went into his living room. Nora and Sid sat on the two dining chairs with their little dog Spot at their feet. He was a forlorn-looking animal with a silly spot of white between his ears. Barker was in his usual dip in the armchair. He slept with one eye shut and watched Spot with the other. I pulled a cushion from behind him, brushed off the dog hairs and put it on the floor.

'That's right, dear,' said Joseph. 'You sit down there. Make yourself at home.'

He poured the tea into pretty floral cups and stepped carefully over Spot to hand them out. He then perched on the edge of the armchair and beamed around the room. The Foxer stared at me from his photograph.

'Isn't this cosy?' said Joseph.

'We were just telling Joseph about our new bungalow,' said Nora. 'Did you know we've moved to Thorncoates?'

I nodded. Thorncoates was the village on the opposite side of the river.

'Their bungalow sounds very smart,' said Joseph. 'It's even got its own garage.'

'Do you still work at Holme Burton, Sid?' I said, trying to sound interested.

'Until the gas pipes are laid. I'm used to moving about Cumberside for my work, but Nora always did her cleaning jobs in Skelland or Holme Burton.'

'Are you going to give them up, Nora?' asked Joseph.

'Yes,' she said. 'I only do Mondays and Wednesdays now, but it's really not practical with no base in Skelland. Sid drops me off each morning at the moment, and we put my bike in the van on Mondays so I can get over to my Holme Burton job in the afternoon, but I've told my ladies that I'll have to stop when Sid finishes at the site.'

'And they're not too happy about *that*,' said Sid proudly. 'It's not easy to get good cleaners these days.'

'Of course I shall feel a bit isolated, all alone in the bungalow,' said Nora, 'but I'll have Spot to keep me company. I feel a bit guilty about leaving the poor darling at home on my work days, but there's a lovely little garden and dry shed for him.'

She lifted Spot up on to her prim knees and kissed him on his wet nose.

This was getting really boring. I just wished they'd go. I wanted to tell Joseph about The Foxer's hat. I wished I'd had the nerve to take it out of the skip. But was it really that important? Surely it would be possible to get hold of another stuffed fox head?

As it happened, it wasn't necessary to tell Joseph. There was a knock at the back door. It was Rib.

'I've come to get Sam,' she said. 'Could you tell her my Mum has given the skip people a rocket and they've promised to come over in half an hour?'

We ran back up Lady Lane. I didn't bother to pretend I wasn't interested.

'It's that fox hat, isn't it?' she said breathlessly.

I nodded. I wasn't very fit. I'd already got a stitch and my mouth was dry.

'I saw you snooping in the skip,' she said. 'I can get the thing out again if you like, but we'll have to make sure my Mum doesn't see it. She's in no mood for foxes, especially not dead ones.'

Rib pulled out the headdress and held it at arm's length.

'Goodness knows why you want it,' she said. 'It gives me the creeps.'

It didn't look nearly so frightening with her there.

'Have you thrown away the black material too?' I said.

'No, Jason's got it. It's a long robe, like a tent. He found something inside it too, like the frame of a bamboo lampshade.'

'Thank goodness it's safe,' I said. 'He'll have to be told he can't keep it though.'

'That could be a problem,' she said. 'He's going to some Spooky Dress Party on Friday and has decided the robe would be useful. I told him he looked hideous enough without a costume. Trust him to get invited to a party. We've hardly been here a second.'

'What about the box?' I said. 'It has to look as if nobody has tampered with it.'

'Jason took it to his room. He's got the robe in it at the moment, but he said he was going to keep his magazines in there after the party. I'll never get him to part with it.'

'Perhaps he'd listen to me.'

Rib looked me up and down.

'Yes, you're probably right,' she said. 'I'll put this creature in the coal house. Go in the back door. Jason's room is up the stairs and first on the right.'

'I know where it is,' I said.

The back door was open. I knocked. There was no answer so I walked into the kitchen, the only private room on the ground floor. A door led from it into a dark hallway. I could hear Mrs Goddard talking on the telephone.

'... yes, it was kind of you to ring, Mr Critchley ... I'd love to come for coffee when we've settled in ... everyone has been so friendly ... Yes, I'll miss the regulars from The Parrot and Silver, of course, but it *does* help to have moved into such a welcoming neighbourhood ... Jason and Rib seem to have survived their first day at school. I was almost more worried about *them*. It's not the first time we've uprooted them and it can be difficult to make friends in a new place ... I'll have to go now. I'm having a skip collected and I can see the lorry has just arrived ... Yes, I'll check no one has tampered with it. It's a good job you rang. Mr Codling said something to me about it and put it on his list of traditional events, but I must admit it had slipped my mind . . .'

I suddenly sensed that I was not alone.

'Heard enough?' said a voice beside me. It was Jason. He was wearing another of his fancy outfits.

'I did knock,' I said lamely.

'And then walked in,' he said. 'I saw you from the garden. Do you make a habit of trespassing in other people's kitchens?'

'Rib said you would be in your room.'

'She's in on it too, is she? I might have known. She can be a real pain. I've just seen her sneaking a bit of junk into the coal house. She is meant to have cleared the place out. Asked you to keep me busy, did she?'

At that moment Rib came in.

'Persuaded him, have you?' she said cheerfully. 'You're not being a bully are you, Jason? I told her she could come up to your room.'

'Nobody goes up to my room without permission,' he said.

'Take no notice,' said Rib. 'He's always pretending to be tough. Watch me make him smile.'

She tickled him playfully in the ribs.

'Get lost,' he said. But he smiled just the same.

'Tell him what he's got to be persuaded about,' said Rib.

'It's to do with Foxing Day,' I said. 'There's a ceremony held in Skelland every September.'

'Foxing Day?' hooted Jason. 'Pull the other one.'

'I know it sounds ridiculous, but it's true. Someone dresses up in a special costume.'

'She's not kidding,' said Rib, although she knew nothing about it.

'It's always been kept at The Fox and Lady,' I said.

'Yes,' said Rib. 'And you've got half of it in your bedroom.'

'*And* the box,' I said. 'We've got the headdress out of the skip.'

'Not that mangy fox head?' said Jason.

'Yes, and you've got to hand over the rest.'

'Who says?'

Mrs Goddard came into the kitchen.

'Hello,' she said, smiling at me. 'And what's your name?'

'She's called Sam,' said Rib.

'I'm sure she can speak for herself, Rebecca. I hope you've offered her a drink or something. I've just got to deal with the skip man. Thank goodness he's here. It will be one less thing to worry about.'

She ran her fingers through her hair.

'Listen, I've just had a Mr Critchley on the phone. He's on some village committee or other and wanted to check we hadn't thrown out a costume they use for a village ceremony. I remember Mr Codling telling me about it. He said it was in a wooden box in a cupboard in the brick shed, and it's to be left well alone until Foxing Day.'

'Don't worry,' said Rib. 'It's safe.'

Her mother bustled out.

'It's time to talk,' said Jason. 'Up to my room, and bring some biscuits.'

He marched on ahead.

'How does he afford so many clothes,' I said. 'I've seen him in three different outfits in the space of two days.'

'He does jobs,' said Rib. 'Paper rounds, shop deliveries and things like that. You've seen nothing yet.'

We found some biscuits and followed Jason. Rib went straight into his room without knocking. He was combing his hair.

'Isn't he vain?' said Rib.

36

'Hasn't anybody taught you to knock?' he said.

Rib ignored the remark. We sat on the bed. The room was very tidy. Several pairs of shoes sat in a neat row under the window and the books were in alphabetical order.

'Her friend used to have this room,' said Rib.

'Really?' said Jason without turning. 'A pity she didn't have better taste in wallpaper. This flowery stuff will have to go.'

'Not until my room's done,' said Rib. 'Mum said mine would be decorated first as you had first choice of room.'

'We'll see about that,' said Jason. 'She only said that to shut you up. Sellotape over the mouth would have been more effective.'

He gave his hair a last flick with the comb before turning to face us.

'What about this Foxing Day rubbish. I think you'd better tell us all about it.'

'It happens on the third Saturday in September,' I said. 'The Skelland Life Committee meets in secret to elect a person to wear the Fox costume for the Ceremony. It is a great honour to be it, and nobody is meant to guess who it is. It creates a bit of interest and people come from the surrounding villages to have a look. It must be quite good for the pub. It starts and finishes here.'

'So what's the problem?' said Jason.

He slid the box from under his desk and pulled out the black robe.

'This will be perfect for my Spooky Dress Party,' he said. 'Look, it's got a sort of frame to fit over my head and shoulders. The headdress must fix on to it somehow.'

'You can't use it,' I said.

'Why not?'

'It would upset some of the older villagers if they got to hear about it,' I said. 'They think it's essential that the ritual is never altered. Call it superstition if you like.'

'No problem,' he said. 'The party is for the Stansholme Youth Club and only younger club members and a guest each can get in. I got an invite from that chap Winston in the fourth year. I doubt if many kids from Skelland will be there. Nobody will recognize it and even if they do they won't care. Besides, I'm not intending to use that flea-ridden fox head. I might catch something.'

He took something else from under his desk. It was a head, made from cleverly folded and glued card.

'Have a look at this,' he said, turning it to face us.

On it was drawn a hideous face, half man, half beast, with wide staring eyes and flared nostrils. The colours were smudged expertly into each other, making it seem alive.

'It's very good,' I said. 'Did you do it?'

'Yes,' he said. 'I used pastel crayons.'

'A self-portrait,' said Rib. 'So what?'

'If I wear this mask with the robes, nobody will guess they're anything to do with Foxing Day,' he said. 'Any objection?'

'I suppose not,' said Rib. 'We'll keep quiet on one condition.'

'Yes?'

'You get us an invitation to the party.'

'I wish you wouldn't use it,' I said. 'Joseph Jenkins would be horrified if he found out.'

'Who on earth is Joseph Jenkins?' said Jason.

'He's that old chap that lives down the lane,' said Rib. 'The one with the dog. Do tell us why you think he'd be so bothered. Whatever has he told you about Foxing Day?'

'I'd rather not say.'

I knew they'd laugh at me.

'She's as superstitious as the rest of them,' said Jason. 'There were two old chaps with dogs in the bar on Saturday. They introduced their dogs, but not themselves. One was called Spot, a miserable looking creature, and the other was Barker. Barker's owner asked if it was still all right for his dog to do tricks. He said the locals liked it. Dad agreed of course. He's soft like that.'

'That's Joseph,' I said. 'I'm glad your Dad agreed. It means a lot to Joseph.'

'If Joseph Jenkins comes in again I'll ask him about this Foxing Day rubbish.'

Rib gave him a warning look.

'I don't see much harm in Jason borrowing the robes, Sam,' she said. 'The party's on Friday. We can keep it to ourselves and put the whole lot back in the box in plenty of time for the ceremony. What they don't know they can't worry about. It can't do any harm, can it?'

Chapter Five

The party was at Stansholme Community Centre. It had been organized by the Youth Club and there would be a disco, a Spooky Dress Competition and food. Club members were allowed to invite one non-member each. Jason had discovered that Baz and Jayne Baldwin were members and persuaded them to let us go. We didn't know what it would be like, but Rib was determined to keep Jason to his word in case he thought he could get away with it next time. My father had agreed to take and collect us, but insisted that we should leave at 10.30 p.m. Jason was not very pleased about that, but a look from Rib soon stopped him complaining.

I decided to go as a ghost (not very original, I know, but it *was* short notice). I wore Mum's old green overall, with a belt to make it short. I had planned to sew strips of crepe paper all over it but Mum dyed an old sheet for me and helped me to sew the strips on. I noticed she put plenty of long strips down the front and back, probably in an effort to cover my legs up a bit. I would have liked to get some green tights, but my pocket money wouldn't run to that, so I made do with some old black ones with black shoes. I had really wanted to go barefoot, but Mum wouldn't hear of it.

I had tucked my hair under a green tinsel wig, painted my nails green (poster paint with clear varnish on top) and was in the process of adding more black and green kohl to my eyes when Rib arrived.

'Brilliant,' she said, 'but why are you green?'

'I'm a *Spectre from the Sea,*' I said in my spookiest voice. 'But why aren't you changed?'

'Because,' she said, 'it's impossible to get Jason out of the bathroom, and the only decent mirror is in there. Don't worry though. I've got my stuff.' She emptied a plastic Tesco bag on to the floor.

'There we are,' she said, pointing to each item in turn. 'Designer sheet (note the hole for my head), bag of flour (self-raising), P.E. shoes and white socks, eye make-up (Mum's) and white gunge for my face and lips borrowed from the school Drama Club's make-up kit (to be returned on Monday).'

'How on earth did you get hold of that?' I said. 'Miss Hathaway never lets anyone get their hands on Drama Club stuff.'

'Asked for her advice, didn't I,' said Rib with a sly grin.

'You'd better get a move on,' I said. 'Dad wants to leave in ten minutes so he can get back in time to watch Gardeners' Realm.'

It didn't take Rib long to get changed.

'There,' she said, after she had pulled the sheet over her head.

'What about your face?'

'Easy,' she said.

41

She peered into the mirror and rubbed the white gunge on to her cheeks, forehead and lips.

'I'm sure that wasn't what Miss Hathaway had in mind,' I said laughing.

'Now the eyes,' she said, drawing a line round them with a black eye pencil and smudging it in a bit.

'Is that it?' I said.

'No,' she said. 'One thing left to do. But first tell me that you've got a vacuum cleaner.'

'We've got a vacuum cleaner.'

'Good,' she said.

She opened the bag of flour and poured it liberally into her hair. She rubbed it well in, gave her hair a shake and walked over to the door. White grains floated down around her like chalk dust.

'Are you coming?' she said. 'We don't want to keep your Dad waiting.'

I followed her obediently, hoping I'd have a chance to vacuum my floor before Mum saw it.

'What *are* you anyway?' I said.

'A *Ghoul from the Grave*,' she said, putting her arms in the air in ghostlike fashion.

Jason was not wearing the robe when we picked him up from The Fox and Lady, though he was completely clothed in black – shoes, socks, jeans and sweatshirt. He carried a huge plastic bag.

'What are you playing at?' said Rib. 'This isn't a trick is it?'

'I'm going to make an entrance,' he said.

'Typical,' said Rib. 'He always has to be the centre of attention.'

Dad dropped us at the Community Centre, making us promise to wait in the foyer when it was time to be collected. It was a dingy place. The window boxes were full of litter and the walls sprayed with graffiti.

Some youths lounged outside on their motor bikes.

42

'Weird,' called the boys, as we climbed out of the car. 'Hey, you with the green wig . . . show us yer legs.'

They laughed derisively. I ignored them. One of them ruffled Rib's ridiculous hair as we walked in.

'I bet she doesn't use Head and Shoulders,' he said.

Jason gave them a cool stare and to my surprise it shut them up.

A bearded man in a woolly sweater greeted us in the foyer.

'Welcome,' he said. 'I'm Brian. And who might you be?'

'We're from Skelland,' said Jason. 'Jason and Rib Goddard, and she's Sam. I'm Winston's guest. Do you know him?'

'I do indeed,' said Brian, his face clouding for a second.

Jason went into the loo to preen himself.

'And we're with Jayne and Baz Baldwin,' said Rib.

'Ah, yes,' he said. 'Jayne and Baz told me to expect you. They came early to help with the refreshments. I call them my "little helpers". They never let me down.'

'Creeps,' said Rib, under her breath.

'What lovely costumes you have made,' he said as he took our money. 'Very spooky. Do go in and join in the fun.'

'I like your weird get-up too,' said Rib.

Brian looked puzzled for a moment.

'Ah,' he said, as realization dawned. 'I think you're teasing me. Very funny.'

He laughed energetically.

'What a dump,' said Rib as we walked into the hall.

'That's because we're too early,' I said. 'It will probably take a while to get going.'

'Pathetic,' she said. 'That bloke with the leather trousers is still rigging up the disco. We used to have *brilliant* discos at my last school. My teacher ran them. He was the best.'

'That's Rory Borealis and his Northern Lights,' I said. 'He's quite well known in Cumbermouth. They only got him for this do because he's Winston's cousin. He agreed to do it for nothing to help raise funds for some new sports equipment.'

'How do you know?' said Rib.

'I heard Winston boasting about it in the dinner queue.'

A lanky girl in a lacy pink creation entwined herself around him.

'What do you think his girlfriend's called,' said Rib, 'Annette Curtin?'

We walked over to Jayne and Baz. They were arranging plates of sausages on sticks.

'Look at the food and squash,' said Rib. 'It's like a kid's party.'

Jayne was dressed as a prim black witch and Baz wore something looking remarkably like school uniform with a set of plastic fangs and a fake scar that was coming off at one end. Rib's mood was getting to me. I was beginning to regret coming.

'Hi fans,' said a voice behind us. 'Where's Jason, man?'

It was Winston.

'He's going to make an entrance,' said Rib. 'What on earth are you meant to be?' Winston was dressed entirely in red with a red-tipped cone of brown wrapping paper on his head.

'I'm a red pencil,' he said.

'What's spooky about that?' said Rib.

'You ever seen a pencil this size?' he said. 'It's spooky all right. Now see me being sharpened.' He twirled round neatly on one foot. His trainers squeaked on the floor.

'You'd better watch it,' said Rib. 'I chew pencils.'

The hall was starting to fill up. There was still no

music and the drifts of witches and skeletons were getting restless.

'Settle down, kids,' called Brian, smiling nervously through his beard. 'Just a slight hitch with the electrics.'

Everyone groaned and someone started singing, 'Why are we waiting?' Others joined in, stamping and clapping in rhythm.

When the lights went out there was a cheer.

Music scorched through the air, vibrating in our ears. The lights flashed into action, darting this way and that. We were all drawn into the centre of the hall, dancing and spinning.

'It's magic,' said Rib, swirling round so that there was a dusty halo of self-raising flour around her head.

'What band is he playing?' I said. 'They're brilliant.'

'Flaming Arrows,' said Winston gyrating past in unpencil-like fashion. 'Wait until you hear the next track. They're heading for the big time. This is cool, real cool.'

The music stopped as abruptly as it had started but the noise still rang in my ears.

'Good evening fans,' said Rory. He put his lips close to the microphone as if he was about to take a bite out of it. 'That was smart moving, kids. Let's stick with Flaming Arrows . . . an instrumental piece. *Like a Fox in the Night.*'

As he spoke the music began to pulse. It was quiet but intense. Bubble patterns in green were projected on to the walls and ceiling making the hall change shape. People stood and swayed.

'Now watch the door, fans,' crooned Rory, mysteriously.

We obeyed. The door slowly opened. Silhouetted against the foyer lights was a tall black figure. As the music crescendoed it strode slowly towards the centre

of the hall. The crowd, still swaying, parted hypnoti-
cally. All eyes watched the masked figure, mirroring
its movements as it began to dance. The eyes in the
mask stared out, the nostrils seemed to breath.

'It's Jason,' gasped Rib, rocking and swaying with
the others. 'But he's so tall.'

The music grew louder, more percussive, and sharp
white lights flashed from the corners of the hall
making shadows leap. Now the figure moved more
vigorously, outstripping its swaying audience. Its
long black robe billowed evilly, swirling angrily as if it
would envelop us all. We clapped rhythmically,
excitedly, urging the figure on. It spun now, round
and round, faster and faster until its features seemed
to blend into each other . . .

It was in the burst of strobe light at the climax of the
piece that we saw it. The figure seemed to spin more
slowly as if its power was spent, and in that moment,
before it fell to the floor, its features melded into those
of a fox.

'Sensational,' said Rory. 'But don't sit down spooks.
Here's Michael Jackson with *Thriller*.'

Jason lay dramatically like a huge grounded bat.

'Get up you idiot,' said Rib. 'It was a great stunt, but
enough's enough.'

There was no reply, or perhaps it was drowned by
the music.

'Come on,' said Rib loudly. 'You made your
entrance. I suppose you got Winston to fix it with Rory
Boring. Can't you be ordinary for a bit like other
people's brothers?'

An arm clutched at her wrist from beneath the thick
robe.

'Get me out of here, Rib,' said Jason's muffled voice.
'Just get me out.'

'He means it Rib,' I said. 'Let's get him up.'

Winston wiggled rhythmically towards us.

'Need any help man?' he said.

'I think Jason's made himself dizzy, the fool,' said Rib. 'That'll teach him not to make appearances. Can you help us dump him on a chair?'

'Sure,' said Winston smoothly.

He deftly slid his arms under Jason's shoulders and dragged him to the side of the hall.

'Let's get his mask off so he can breathe.'

He tugged at the mask. It came off, but Jason's face was not inside it.

'Blimey,' said Winston. 'A fake head. I thought his shoulders were in a funny place.'

'No wonder the idiot looked so tall,' said Rib. 'He's wearing that frame. There's some thin material over the front so he can see out.'

'I think we should get this robe off him,' I said. 'He must be sweltering in there.'

The three of us hauled him up and dragged the heavy material up over his head. He slumped back on to the chair. He looked a bit green, but perhaps it was the lighting.

'A drink,' he said. 'Get me a drink and some air.'

We helped him into the foyer, and Winston went in search of squash.

Two orange squashes later Jason spoke.

'I should never have worn that thing,' he said. 'Not for dancing.'

'Do you need any help?' said Brian from his table by the door. He had been joined now by two other men in warm woollies.

'He's fine,' said Rib. 'He just got a bit dizzy.'

'Get me out of here,' said Jason, under his breath. 'Ask him to ring Sam's Dad, to see if he'll fetch us.'

'Don't be a spoilsport, Jason,' said Rib. 'We don't want to go home just because you can't take the pace.'

'I think there's more to it than that, Rib,' I said. 'Something odd happened out there. You saw the fox didn't you?'

'Yes, a trick of the light, so what?'

'It was no trick,' said Jason. 'When I was out there I *was* The Fox.'

Chapter Six

It was impossible to discuss things on the way home from the party and Dad was in a foul temper because he'd been called out in the middle of his programme.

'We're very sorry about this, Mr Hinch,' said Rib. 'Jason was taken poorly and we thought it best if we all came home together.'

Jason said nothing and Dad had grunted something about cloches.

We stopped outside The Fox and Lady.

'When shall I see you?' I said, as they climbed out of the car.

'Tomorrow morning,' said Rib.

We met in Jason's room. The wooden box stood in the middle of the floor.

'It's all in there,' said Jason. 'Headdress, robes and frame. When do they collect it?'

'Not until Foxing Day. Are you sure you have put it back as you found it?'

'Positive.'

'Good,' I said. 'We must get it back into the shed cupboard without being seen.'

'We can do it under cover of darkness,' said Jason, 'though I can't really see what all the fuss is about.'

'Listen who's talking,' said Rib. 'What about the fuss *you* made last night?'

Jason looked uncomfortable.

'What did you mean when you said you *were* The Fox?' I said.

'Just that I'd done a brilliant bit of acting,' he said.

'That's not how it sounded to me,' said Rib. 'I'd like to know a bit more about this fox story.'

'It's a load of rubbish,' said Jason.

'Sam and I know what we saw when you were dancing, don't we?' she said.

'It was probably just a trick of the light,' I said.

'What are you talking about?' said Jason.

'Your head looked like a fox,' said Rib. 'It was really weird.'

Jason laughed unconvincingly.

'You're mad,' he said.

'Tell us more about this Foxing business, Sam,' said Rib.

I shook my head.

'I'm going to ask Joseph Jenkins about it,' said Rib. 'Then we'll see if I'm mad. Are you two coming with me or not?'

We could tell it was no good arguing with her.

Joseph was at home.

'Brought your friends to meet me, have you?' he said. 'You're lucky to catch me here. I've just got back from digging over the Baldwins' vegetable patch.'

Joseph had taken to doing occasional odd jobs in the village since retiring.

'Why can't Baz and Jayne do it?' muttered Jason.

'They probably don't like getting their Paddington Bear wellies muddy,' said Rib.

'We could come over another time if you're tired,' I said.

'Wouldn't hear of it,' said Joseph. 'Come in and have a cup of tea.'

He showed us into his living room and went into the kitchen to put the kettle on. Barker, who was lounging on the armchair, opened his eyes briefly as his nose registered unfamiliar smells.

'What a tip,' said Jason, looking round the cluttered walls.

'It's beautiful,' said Rib. 'I love all his stuff.'

'Please don't ask him about Foxing Day,' I whispered. 'He'll guess something's wrong.'

Soon Joseph came back with a tray. He'd put out his best china cups, his cat-shaped tea pot and a plate of Bourbon biscuits.

'I'm Rib and he's Jason,' said Rib, helping herself to a biscuit and squeezing next to Barker on the armchair. 'We're from the pub.'

'Pleased to meet you both,' he said, pulling out the dining chairs for Jason and me. 'I think I saw young Jason looking into the bar the other night. How are you settling in?'

'OK,' said Rib. 'I do like your house. All these bits and pieces are lovely.'

'Thank you, lass. There aren't many who appreciate such things. I'll tell you about my hobby room one day.'

I felt a twinge of jealousy. Jason said nothing. Joseph pulled the low stool from under the table and sat down.

'Perhaps you'd better tell me what's the matter,' he said.

'Who says there's something the matter?' said Jason rudely.

'I've known young Sam long enough to be able to tell when something's bothering her. She wasn't very happy the last time I saw her either. What is it love?'

The kindness in his voice made me feel like crying.

'I'm missing Emma,' I said.

'We'll soon cheer her up,' said Rib.

Joseph's face clouded for a moment. He didn't like to see me unhappy. Rib took another Bourbon and crunched it noisily.

'What's that funny picture?' she said innocently. 'The one with the fox head?'

'That's to do with Foxing Day,' said Joseph.

'My Mum said something about it,' she said. 'Isn't the costume at our place?'

'Aye, it's always been kept there. I trust your parents will agree to things going as they should.'

'Is it important?'

'Very important. Mr Codling will have told your parents all about it.'

'Oh dear,' said Rib. 'I'm not sure they understand. It was on a list of traditional events, along with darts fixtures. It doesn't matter what date it's on does it?'

Joseph blanched.

'Don't worry,' said Rib. 'I can easily put them right. It must be good business for the pub. They'll like that. But could you tell me about it so that I can explain?'

'I can see I'll have to,' said Joseph. 'We can't have it treated as a fun day. But promise not to chat too freely about it. Just tell your parents as much as they need to know.'

'I promise,' said Rib.

'It all started many years ago,' said Joseph. 'There

was a bit of rough land on Lady Lane, where your pub stands. A gypsy lady used to come there every summer. She had a painted caravan, pulled by her old horse. Every June she'd arrive, and every September she left. The chap who owned the land was called Ezekiel Cooper. He wasn't bothered about her. She made no mess and helped him on the farm to repay his hospitality. His farm really seemed to thrive when she was around.

'But the other villagers felt differently, especially the farm workers' families that lived in these cottages. They resented her taking their work and were afraid of her too. She never revealed her name and it was rumoured that she had secret powers. Children were told to have nothing to do with her.'

'What about The Fox?' said Rib.

'She kept a fox as a pet. It was so tame that she could train it to do tricks. The villagers wanted to get rid of her and blamed her for anything that went wrong in the area. If anything was stolen, they said her fox had taken it and if a cow fell ill, they said she'd cast a spell on it.

'She was very striking to look at and, although she did some heavy work on Cooper's farm, she never seemed to age. When she wasn't working she wore a long white robe and adorned herself with jewellery. They called her a witch.'

'Our place must have been named after her,' said Rib.

'That's right.'

'Why don't they show her face on the pub sign?'

'There was a great hoo-ha about the sign. Some of the older villagers said she'd be able to watch them if her face was shown.'

'What happened to her?' said Rib.

'She outstayed her welcome, lass. Come one

September she showed no sign of leaving. Cooper was quite happy for her to stay. He had good luck when she was around. Her horse was ailing and she said she was so happy in Skelland she didn't see why she should leave. There was a spate of mishaps around that time. Children were sick, one even died, and things went missing. Chickens were stolen, and ladies' jewellery disappeared from their houses without any evidence of a break-in, and these things happened as far away as Holme Burton.

'Being unable to explain the mishaps the villagers blamed the gypsy lady. Some folks got together and decided to scare her off. They went down to her caravan one night. I don't think they meant to harm her at first, but things got out of hand. The Lady refused to come out of her caravan to listen to them. They said they'd wait as long as it took and lit themselves a fire.

'She didn't come out. She just stood at her window and stared calmly out at them. There was a man there whose little girl was sick. He was scared for her life. He panicked. "Let's burn her out," he said, and before they knew what they were doing they had rolled her caravan over the flames. She came out then, with her fox in her arms, but no one reasoned with her as they had planned. They were dumbstruck by her beauty and terrified by the forgiveness in her face.

'"I see it's time for me to leave," she said. "But my spirit will live on."'

'Where did she go?' said Rib.

'She walked down the lane to the river. Most were too scared to move, but one young lad followed her down there and he told what happened next. There used to be a small boat there in those days with a rope fixed across the river and folks used to pull themselves across. It was hard work, though. That river's got a fair pull to it. The boat was on the Skelland side. She pushed in her fox, climbed into it and began to haul herself across the river, but as she got further from the bank it was hard for the lad to see her. He thought she might have disappeared, or perhaps she slid into the water, but he was certain that she never reached the other side. No trace of the boat, The Lady or The Fox was ever found.'

'What happened to her caravan?' said Rib.

'They pulled it off the fire and doused the flames and later they searched it through. The funny thing was that there was no trace of any of the stolen property in there. She had spirited it all away with her. The caravan stood on the field for weeks until eventually someone broke it up for firewood.'

'Did all the burglaries stop after she disappeared?' said Jason.

'No, lad, things went from bad to worse. The illness and thefts continued.'

'It can't have been the gypsy lady then,' said Rib.

'It was her all right. Her spirit lived on just as she had said . . . and there were sightings to prove it.'

'Never,' scoffed Jason.

'It's true, lad. People saw her at night. She was clothed in white and floated across the river as if she were standing in a boat. The strange thing is that she never reached the other side. She disappeared just as the gypsy lady did that night. Nobody ever crossed the river there again.'

'What happened to Ezekiel Cooper?' I asked.

'He upped and left shortly after she disappeared. He sold his land off. Someone bought part of it and built your pub and the semi-detached houses on Elm Street. Farmer Williams took on the farm buildings and the rest of the land, but he didn't prosper. The families moved out of these cottages. There was not enough work for them and they were too afraid to stay.'

'What about The Fox?' said Jason. 'I suppose they saw its ghost tiptoeing around the village with a swag bag over its shoulder.'

'It was seen all right. Some people even took shots at it, but it always escaped. It was only when they decided to fight fox with fox that things settled down in Skelland. They called in a wise old man called Abraham Johnson. He said the villagers should unite to fight the evil. It was a year since The Fox and Lady had disappeared. They had a ceremony on the third Saturday that September, close to the date when they had disappeared. A committee of four was formed, with three people from Skelland and one from Holme Burton. A costume was made and the word went out that someone was needed to wear it.'

'Did many people want to do it?' asked Rib.

'There was only one volunteer. His identity was kept secret, and if the villagers guessed who it was, they said nothing. That way there would be no danger of him being victimized by evil spirits.'

'What did he have to do?' she said.

'He danced,' said Joseph. 'A band was formed and The Foxer danced all around the village to ward off the evil.'

'Did it work?' said Rib.

'Aye, lass. From that day onward they were free from trouble. Both Fox and Lady were never seen again.'

'Why do they still have Foxing Day then?' asked Rib.

'We repeat the ceremony every September, to make sure it stays that way. Ruby and I would never have moved in here had we not been sure of that.'

'Who is on the committee now?' said Jason.

'I am,' said Joseph gravely, 'I was asked to join when I retired from my job in Cumbermouth.'

'Who else?' asked Rib.

'Den Critchley from Skelland and Mr Carpenter from Holme Burton.

'Sid was on it until recently. He had to give up his seat on the committee when he moved. Mrs Mycroft, wife of the village scoolteacher has taken his place. He took it very badly, did Sid. He refused to give up his seat at first, though he knew that members have always come from Skelland or Holme Burton. We told him something could go wrong if he stayed. He said he thought things would go wrong if he left, especially as he was being replaced by a woman. I thought he'd never forgive us for voting him out and Nora gave up her cleaning job at the Critchleys' as a protest.'

'They seemed friendly enough the other day,' I said.

'They accepted it in the end,' said Joseph. 'I'm glad. I wouldn't have liked to lose them as friends.'

'I bet you get loads of volunteers to wear the costume now,' said Rib.

'Anyone over the age of twenty-one can submit his name to the committee,' said Joseph. 'Then a choice is made.'

'Then what happens?' said Jason.

'There's a brick shed behind your pub, and that's where the chosen person puts his costume on. The costume stays untouched in there until the day. It's padlocked in a box and kept in a locked cupboard, not that it would be in anyone's interest to tamper with it. If anything were to change, the evil might return.'

'What if it needed repairs?' asked Rib.

'It has remained intact for years and they say it has never been in anyone's home since it was made. The original landlord of the pub was quite happy to go along with it, as he'd had bad luck like everyone else.

The best beer went off as soon as he took on the pub, and he had to throw it down the drains.'

'What if someone got the costume out by mistake?' asked Jason.

'Bad would come of it, lad.'

'We'll make sure it's OK,' said Rib. 'By the way, is this your whistle?'

She pulled a long slim whistle out of her pocket.

'I found it outside your place last week.'

'No, lass. That's a dog whistle. I don't need anything like that for Barker. We've got a rapport.'

'I'm looking forward to seeing his tricks,' said Rib, treating Joseph to her most winning smile.

'I think it's time to go,' I said.

'You've been very quiet, Sam,' said Joseph as we left.

'Let's go down the lane,' said Rib as soon as we were out of Joseph's gate. 'I want to see where the ferry boat was.'

'I walked down there the other day,' said Jason. 'There's nothing to see.'

But he followed nevertheless.

We walked towards the river. The tarmac deteriorated at the end of the lane into stone and weed, then petered out to a muddy track that cut up the dyke at the riverside.

We climbed up. The tide was low, leaving an expanse of brown mud on either side.

'Not very picturesque is it?' said Jason.

He threw a chunk of stone into the mud. It sank in leaving a pock mark.

'You've got no imagination,' said Rib. 'Can't you just see the lady in white floating across the water to her doom?'

'Do you have to joke about it?' I said.

'I didn't know Skelland had a history,' she said. 'The

first time I saw the place I thought it was a real dump.'

'Well some of us happen to like it,' I said.

I strode crossly along the dyke in the direction of Cumbermouth.

'Wait for us,' said Rib. 'Where are you going?'

'I'm going home,' I said.

'Can we get home this way?' said Rib, stumbling after me in her effort to keep up.

'If you like,' I said. 'The track goes all the way to Cumbermouth but we can get off it at Finn Lane and get back to Elm Street that way.'

Jason followed us, occasionally hurling missiles into the water. A small motor boat chugged by, rainbowing the water's surface with petrol.

'Look,' said Rib as she climbed over the stile at the edge of Lady Meadow. 'There's a good view of the back of the pub from here. I can even see the tea towels on the washing line.'

'Can't we get back across the field?' said Jason. 'This river is truly boring.'

'It's Mr Broadway's field,' I said. 'He can't stop us walking along here, but he appears from nowhere if anyone puts a foot off the dyke.'

'It doesn't belong to a Williams any more then,' said Rib.

I was surprised she remembered the name.

'Joseph says it's had one owner after another,' I said. 'They try different ways of using the land, but it never pays.'

'I'm not surprised,' said Rib. 'They seem to be growing thistles and dandelions at the moment.'

When we got back to The Fox and Lady, Jason led us down to the shed. It was carelessly built, with cement bulging from between the bricks like butter icing.

Jason went in first.

'Notice the beautifully swept floor,' he said. 'I made a much better job of this than Rib did of the coal hole.'

Rib pulled a face behind his back.

Tools were piled up against one wall, and a lawn mower on the other.

'Is this your stuff?' I said.

'Yes, the Codlings left a few bits and pieces, but they were mainly junk.'

A large cupboard was fixed to the back wall. Old green paint was flaking off its doors.

'Here is the cupboard,' said Jason obviously.

He pulled the doors open.

'And here is the shelf.'

'Don't be sarcastic,' said Rib.

'Follow me,' said Jason.

We went out into the garden, behind the shed, and looked over the wall towards the river.

'I bet I could get over that field at night,' said Jason.

'Why would anyone want to do that?' said Rib.

'To get to the brick shed unseen,' said Jason. 'It can't be that difficult to get over the back wall.'

'The only person who's shown any interest in our shed recently is you,' said Rib.

'Not so,' said Jason. 'Old Joseph Jenkins said the box was padlocked and locked in a cupboard. It was in the cupboard all right but the cupboard was wide open.'

'Yes, and you ripped a padlock off the box. How are you going to put that back?'

'I'm not going to put it back,' he said. 'Because there *was* no padlock. And you know what that means, don't you?'

'Yes,' I said grimly. 'Someone got there before you.'

'Are you sure the doors weren't locked?' said Rib.

'Positive,' said Jason. 'Neither was the Fox Box.'

'So someone came into the shed, unlocked the cupboard and ripped a padlock off the box,' I said.

'Why would anyone want to do that?'

'*How* could anyone do it,' said Rib. 'You can see the shed from the house, and the garden is lit at night and locked after hours.'

'Not every night,' said Jason. 'What about the night before we arrived? Perhaps the stand-in bar staff forgot!'

'They could have got in through the car park, or from the riverside,' I said. 'But if they went to the trouble of doing that, why not *take* the costume?'

'It depends on their motive,' said Jason. 'Just imagine if one of the old villagers had annoyed someone. That someone might decide to tamper with the cupboard, knowing that whoever came to get the costume on Foxing Day would have a fit.'

'Surely nobody *really* believes in all that rubbish?' said Rib.

'Joseph does,' I said. 'Though I can't imagine anyone wanting to upset him.'

'What about the chap that rang Mum?'

'Mr Critchley? Nobody likes him,' I said. 'He'd go mad if he found the cupboard open.'

'We'll be able to see *how* mad next Saturday,' said Jason.

'Whatever do you mean?' said Rib. 'You are going to put the Fox Box back, aren't you?'

'Yes,' he said. 'Exactly as I found it . . . an open box in an open cupboard.'

Chapter Seven

We did it that evening. Rib went downstairs ahead of us to make sure the coast was clear, Jason carried the box down and I gave back up cover. We got to the shed without being seen and shut the door behind us. I persuaded Jason not to switch on the light. The garden lights shone through the window so he could easily see enough to push the box into the cupboard and shut the doors.

'That's the end of that,' said Jason.

There was a trace of relief in his voice as he turned to leave.

'Shh,' said Rib. 'There's someone outside.'

'It's The Fox,' said Jason, rolling his eyes. 'Prepare to meet your doom.'

This gave Rib a fit of giggles.

There was a scratching noise outside the door and the catch clicked open. Sid's dog Spot put his sad nose into the gap and pushed his way in, wagging his tail so hard that his body wagged as well.

'Out, damned Spot!' said Jason, pointing theatrically to the door.

They were doing Macbeth in Year Four. I wished he would be serious. Rib giggled uncontrollably and Spot wagged his tail even harder.

We heard a voice from outside the garden gate.

'Where's the little beggar got to?'

It was Sid.

'Be quiet,' I said. 'We don't want to be found in here.'

Rib stuffed the sleeve of her sweatshirt in her mouth and carried on laughing in silence. Jason picked up the wagging dog around his middle and put him down by the door.

'Out, I say,' he said, nudging him with the toe of his shoe.

'There you are, you young scoundrel,' called Sid. 'Come here boy. It's time to watch Barker's tricks!'

Jason peered through the gap in the door.

'He's gone,' he said. 'And the old chap can't have seen us.'

Rib took her sleeve out of her mouth and inhaled loudly.

'Now what?' I said.

'We go in of course,' said Rib weakly. 'Barker's about to perform.'

'I must see this,' said Jason. 'Does he do juggling?'

We peered into the bar from the hall, pulling the velvet door curtain nearly shut so as not to draw attention to ourselves. Joseph and Barker were on the far side of the bar. Chairs and tables had been pulled back so that everybody could see. Joseph took a long drink of beer. It left bubbles on his lip.

'What'll it be then, Ladies and Gentlemen?' he said.

'Do some sums with him,' called someone.

'Very well,' said Joseph. 'Let's have some hush so as he can concentrate.'

'Quick,' whispered Jason. 'Take notes. It'll save us time with our Maths homework.'

Rib got the giggles again. She was being very silly.

'Now then, Barker,' said Joseph seriously. 'What's two and two?'

Barker barked four times. The crowd cheered and Barker ran around in happy circles.

'What number comes after four?' said Joseph.

Barker barked five times.

This went on for several minutes, with Joseph putting the questions and Barker getting the answers right.

'He's better at Maths than you,' said Jason to Rib.

'He's better looking than you,' she said.

'Have a drink on the house, Joseph,' said Mr Goddard.

'Not for me thanks,' said Joseph. 'But Barker's partial to a glass of ale. That's his tankard up there.'

The drink was passed over and Barker lapped it up enthusiastically.

'Ugh,' said Rib. 'I hope they don't wash his tankard up with the other stuff.'

'Joseph's very particular about that,' I said. 'He takes it to the cloakroom tap and does it himself.'

'And for the final question,' announced Joseph dramatically. 'Tell us how many children are peeping through the red curtain.'

'He'll never get that right,' said Jason. 'The rest was a trick. He can't have prepared him for this.'

Barker barked three times. I moved away from the door, not wishing to be discovered and Rib followed, but Jason, who loved an audience, pulled the curtain open, stepped forward and took a bow.

'Wrong,' he said. 'There's just one of me.'

Barker barked three times.

'That's not what the dog thinks, lad,' said Joseph.

Jason shrugged.

'Come on girls,' he said pulling us into the doorway. 'Barker knows best.'

The crowd cheered and for a moment Joseph looked triumphant.

Chapter Eight

I stayed at home on Sunday. After I had completed my Science assignment I tried to write to Emma, but the words wouldn't come. I should have written it earlier as Mrs Dean had suggested, but things had changed since Emma left and I wasn't sure how to tell her about them.

When I got home from school on Monday there was a pink envelope waiting for me. In it was a letter from Emma. I took it up to my room to read. The twins had got their stereo on again. I was tempted to rap on the wall, but experience told me that it would only make them put up the volume.

The Red Lion,
Queen Street,
Victoria Road,
Belbroughton.
Friday 8th

Dear Sam,

Sorry I haven't written sooner. Things have been a bit hectic here. I've been sorting out my new room.

It's quite a bit bigger, but the view isn't so good. We're in a built-up area so all I can see are other people's gardens. I wish there was somewhere to walk like Lady Lane. The nearest bit of open ground is Victoria Park, but that's always full of kids.

Do write and tell me what's happening in Skelland. What is Year Three like at school? Does Miss Stark give you lots of homework? My school is just down the road. It's called Queen Street Middle. My teacher is very funny. His name is Mr Green and he keeps making us laugh. I sit next to a girl called Emily and he gets our names mixed up. As long as he gives me Emily's good marks I don't mind. She's really brainy, but quite nice all the same. I went for tea with her today. Her mother makes delicious cakes. She even gave me a huge hunk of chocolate cake to bring home. I'd send you some, only it might make the envelope sticky!

My Gran is still poorly. I call in to see her on the way home from school. Mum and Dad are glad they've been able to move closer to her, but they miss the regulars from The Fox and Lady. What are the new people like? I'm dying to hear all about them. I miss everybody, especially you. Please write soon and tell me everything that has been happening.

lots of love
from Emma

I answered her letter straight away.

34 Elm Street,
Skelland,
Cumberside.
Monday 11th

Dear Emma,

Thanks for your letter. I see you are still trying to use up the pink paper your Gran gave you! I hope she's feeling a bit better now. Do give her my love.

Things have been hectic here too. School is pretty much the same (worst luck!). Miss Stark is OK but she hasn't got much of a sense of humour, something you need with the Kilby twins in your class. We get heaps of homework. Each teacher seems to think she is the only one giving us any and so we get a week's worth every night.

I'm not speaking to Isabelle again. She really fancies herself. I told her it was a pity nobody else did. That didn't go down very well as she has a crush on Winston. As if he'd give her a second look!

The pub seems really odd without you. I've met the new people. It's a pity you didn't see them when they looked round the place. They have a girl and a boy. The boy is called Jason. He really gets on my nerves. He thinks he's God's gift to the world. He's in 4B at school. He's got friendly with Winston and is nearly as vain as he is. Worst of all, he's got your old room. The girl is our age. She's called Rib (short for Rebecca) and is as thin as a runner bean. She sits next to me at school and keeps asking questions, especially in Maths.

Must go now. Supper's ready. Mum's already called twice. Write soon.

Love from
Sam

P.S. We've got swimming this term. It's awful. We trek to the pool, right through Stansholme shopping arcade, arrive exhausted, do a thousand lengths (with swimming hat on!), trek back (in a crocodile) and spend the rest of the morning with wet hair dripping down our necks.

'What kept you?' said Mum, when I finally got to the kitchen. Her face was pink from leaning over the oven and she looked a bit cross.

'Sorry, Mum, I was just writing to Emma.'

'I hope you've done your homework, young lady,' said Dad. 'There's been too much gallivanting about recently.'

He still hadn't forgiven me for the party incident.

'Leave her alone,' said Mum. 'She's got to make new friends now Emma's gone. There's more to life than work.'

'You'll not say that if she gets a bad report.'

'She's never had a bad one yet.'

'There's always a first time.'

I sat down and kept quiet. Mum held a plate of sausage and chips in front of me. The sausages gleamed with grease.

'Did you tell Emma all about your new friends?' she said.

'Nearly all,' I said.

Chapter Nine

Something very strange happened the next week. It was Wednesday. Mrs Dean was away with laryngitis so we had no Science homework. Rib, who hated Science, had invited me round to The Fox and Lady that evening to celebrate. We went up to her room. It was a dismal place. Emma's parents had used it as a spare room and had never got round to decorating it. The wallpaper had gone yellow and the carpet was threadbare like an unfinished tapestry.

'Horrid, isn't it?' said Rib.

We sat on the edge of her bed.

'Pretty awful,' I agreed.

She had cadged a bag of crisps each from the bar. We munched for a while in silence. Eventually Rib sighed and walked over to her window.

'The view's not much better,' she said. 'All I get to see are cars parking.'

'I like watching the sky,' I said.

She pulled a face.

'There *is* no sky tonight,' she said.

It was a dark evening with a hint of mist in the air.

'Let's pray for rain tomorrow,' she said. 'Anything to get out of Games.'

'What's wrong with Games?' I said.

'Isabelle Podd keeps "accidentally" kicking me on the ankles when we practise ball skills.'

'If it's not outside we'll go in the gym instead,' I said.

'Let's pray the gym floods then.'

She peered more intently out of the window.

'I don't believe it,' she said. 'Something else is moving out there. And to think I thought I'd got the most boring view in the universe.'

I stood beside her, aware again of how slight she was. A small light was jerking its way up Lady Lane.

'It's someone with a torch,' I said. 'It could be Joseph, but he usually works in his hobby room until later than this.'

The light jerked nearer. As it came closer to The Fox and Lady a car pulled round into the car park. In the beam from its headlights we saw a tense running figure. It was Joseph, with Barker racing along beside him.

'He's on the run,' said Rib. 'Joseph Jailbird has nicked something from the building site.'

'Don't be ridiculous,' I said.

Rib grinned. She enjoyed teasing me.

'He's only holding the torch,' I said. 'What do you think he's taken? A pocketful of sand?'

'No,' she said. 'He probably took a breeze block but had to drop it and run when they spotted him. Let's hope it didn't land on his toe. I bet he comes into the pub for sanctuary. Let's go down and see what he's up to.'

We ran down to the hall and pulled back the door curtain a little so that we could see into the bar. Joseph was standing in the middle of the room. His chest heaved from running and his face was drawn and white. Barker whined up at his distraught master and the bar fell silent.

'What's up Joseph?' said Mr Goddard. 'You look as if you've seen a ghost.'

'The Lady's back,' said Joseph. His voice was a taut whisper. 'She's back and we're *all* doomed.'

Someone drew him towards the fire and sat him in a chair. Barker sat anxiously beside him. Mr Goddard fetched him a brandy and everyone listened to hear what he would say next.

'I never thought I'd see the day,' he said. 'She was there on the river all in white. She floated across in the mist as if she was standing in a boat, but she didn't reach the other side. She slid down into the river just as she did all those years ago.'

He gulped some brandy down. The fire spat out a few red sparks as the coals settled.

'Her spirit was never at rest. It's been trapped between worlds ... and now someone's let it out again...'

'Come on Joseph,' said Mr Goddard kindly. 'Drink up and you'll soon feel better.'

'Better?' said Joseph numbly. 'No, sir ... I'll not feel better ... We're doomed.'

Some youths by the dart board sniggered.

72

'Give it a rest Grandad,' said one of them.

People started talking again.

Sid Hambly walked over to Joseph. Nora was not with him.

'I'll bet someone's tampered with the box. I knew something like this would happen,' he said. 'Let's get Den Critchley over and see what's to be done. I'll go ring him.'

'Come on,' said Rib, tugging my sleeve. 'We'd better warn Jason they're on to him.'

Jason was at his desk, drawing.

'What do *you* want?' he said, without looking up. 'If you want to borrow some of my tapes again the answer's no.'

'It's nothing like that,' said Rib. 'Joseph Jenkins has seen a ghost and they've sent for Mr Critchley to see if the box has been tampered with.'

'So?'

'Please come,' I said.

'You want me to stop drawing just because some old chap has drunk too much?'

'They're bound to go to the shed,' said Rib. 'They'll see the cupboard is open and the Fox Box padlock is missing. Mum and Dad will tell them you cleaned it out and then they'll be up here asking questions.'

'So?'

Rib tried another approach.

'Well *I'm* not missing out on this. I'd love to see this Critchley chap's face when he gets here. Come on Sam. Let's get down there.'

Jason sighed.

'I suppose I'd better come and make sure you don't put your foot in it,' he said.

We sat at the kitchen table.

'Look cool,' said Rib, pretending to read the evening paper.

'That won't fool them,' said Jason. 'Everyone knows you can't read.'

'Shut up you two,' I said. 'Let's hear what they say.'

Den Critchley arrived in under ten minutes. We heard footsteps and serious voices in the hall.

'They're coming through this way,' said Rib excitedly.

Den was wearing a dark suit and tie. His grey hair was swept back from his forehead making him look like Count Dracula. He took a tangle of keys from his suit pocket and rattled them like bones. Mr Goddard, Sid Hambly and Joseph were with him, plus Spot and Barker.

'What's going on, Dad?' asked Rib innocently.

'Never you mind,' he said. 'Haven't you kids got any homework to do?'

He turned to the other men.

'It's a busy night gentlemen. I hope this little expedition is not going to take long. I've a business to run.'

'Where are you going, Dad?' asked Jason.

'We're going to have a look in the brick shed. I hope you haven't been mucking about with anything in there.'

Jason managed to look offended and Rib pretended she hadn't heard. She ran her finger round and round a coffee stain on the table.

The men and dogs were back in less than ten minutes. Their faces were grim.

'What's up?' asked Jason.

Joseph sank shakily on to a stool. His arms hung limply by his side.

'The box has been tampered with,' he said. 'That's what's up.'

Barker nuzzled his wet nose into Joseph's hand.

74

'What do you know about this, Jason?' said Mr Goddard irritably. 'I should never have let you clear out that shed.'

'What *do* you mean?' said Jason.

Den Critchley brought his face down to Jason's level and spoke very slowly through gleaming teeth.

'Someone has broken into a cupboard and forced a box open,' he said. 'And *we* want to find that someone.'

'Does it matter?' said Joseph sadly. 'The harm's done. There'll be no stopping The Lady now.'

Jason stood. Rib and I could tell he was about to go dramatic again.

'I presume,' he said, looking Den Critchley straight in the eye, 'that you are talking about the box with a mouldy fox head in it?'

'*You* opened it?' said Sid.

'Yes,' said Jason. 'I opened the cupboard and took out the box. My parents had told me to clear out the shed and I wanted to see if there was anything worth keeping in there.'

'I didn't say anything about breaking into cupboards and forcing padlocks,' said Mr Goddard.

'I didn't *have* to break in,' said Jason. 'Neither the cupboard nor the box was locked.'

'Someone had been there before you?' said Mr Goddard. He looked accusingly at Rib.

'It wasn't me,' said Rib. 'And I know Mum didn't do because Mr Critchley rang to remind her about it. Anyway, why is the thing kept in a shed if it's that important? Anybody could get to it if they wanted.'

'Those locks weren't strong ones,' said Joseph. 'They were symbolic. Nobody in the history of Kelland would have wanted to break them.'

Sid nodded.

'Somebody did,' said Den, his eyebrows bristling.

75

'And they must have had their reasons.'

'I thought you had the only keys,' said Sid. 'And we know you wouldn't have done it.'

'There's been spirits at work,' said Joseph.

Barker whined sympathetically.

Mrs Goddard put her head round the door.

'Have you finished playing detectives?' she said irritably. 'There's a bar full of customers that need serving *and* we're out of smoky bacon crisps.'

'Just coming, dear,' said Mr Goddard.

He turned to Den.

'We can't undo what's been done, Mr Critchley,' he said. 'Surely it's best to forget about the incident. There's no point in letting this go any further. The less said about it the better. We don't want to worry anybody unnecessarily. We know Joseph *thought* he saw something, but it could easily have been a trick of the mist on the river.'

'I know what I saw,' said Joseph.

'Joseph's not one to mistake a thing like that,' said Sid. 'I don't know what my Nora will have to say about all this.'

'If The Lady's about,' said Jason looking at each man in turn, 'what about The Fox?'

'That, young man,' said Den, 'remains to be seen.'

Chapter Ten

On Friday night I was woken by a storm. Rain
hammered on the roof and made the gutters rush and
gurgle. I went over to my window to watch the
lightning. It lit the world with white and made the
dark shadows of trees and houses leap and lurch. For a
split second, as all was light, I thought I saw a fox,
splashing down the road towards Lady Lane, with its
head held high and its tail as bushy as if it were dry. It
must have been a trick of light or the remnants of a
dream. Soon the thunder came rattling over the sky
and I ran back to the warmth of my bed.

I could hear that it had stopped raining when I woke
the next morning. I looked out of my bedroom
window. It was windy and uneasy clouds raced across
the sky. The road was still wet and a soft silt of mud
leaned up against the kerb.

Clive Mycroft, the village schoolteacher, was already out there with Jason. They were hanging the last of the Foxing Day bunting along the street. Jason held the ladder against a lamppost while Clive knock-kneed his way up it. He was a nice man, but not very practical. They would have done better to get his wife Angela to see to it. She was both practical and confident. She had turned the downstairs of the schoolhouse into a studio where she made pots and weird sculptures. Mr Mycroft always looked rather embarrassed if she turned up for school functions as she never bothered to tidy her long hair, which was pinned up on her head like a half-hearted bird's nest. Neither did she change out of one of the home-printed, swirly dresses which she wore at home.

Jason should have volunteered to go up the ladder but he was probably too selfish to think of that. He felt me watching him and grinned up at me instead of making sure Mr Mycroft was all right.

'Lazybones,' he called.

I pretended I hadn't noticed him and shut my curtains firmly.

Breakfast was a silent affair. My parents seemed to be annoyed with each other, probably because the storm had kept them awake for half the night.

'They're putting the bunting up,' I said.

'Let's hope they take it down properly,' said Dad. 'I've only just got the last knot of tinsel out of our copper beech and that was from the Christmas before last.'

'Is it all right if I have lunch at The Fox and Lady?' I said.

There was no answer.

'They're laying on a hot dog barbecue before the Foxing starts.'

Dad grunted.

'Is there any chance of having my pocket money?'
Mum tutted.

'Well I haven't had any for three weeks,' I said. 'I'm skint.'

Silence.

'I shall assume that if nobody grunts or tuts it's all right to take some cash from Mum's purse.'

Nick and Dean were whizzing round the car park on their bikes when I got to The Fox and Lady. I had offered to help the Goddards set out the equipment for the barbecue so I went into their garden by the back gate. They had rigged up a green tarpaulin. It lurched and flapped in the wind. Beneath it were some wooden trestle tables and the barbecue. Mr Goddard was arranging trays of rolls, sausages and sliced onion while Mrs Goddard brought out piles of plates and cutlery.

Rib came out of the back door. She looked even scruffier than usual and her hair stood out in greasy spikes.

'Excuse my hair,' she said, grinning. 'I tried some of Jason's gunge on it last night and it's still in shock. Have you come to help?'

I nodded.

'How did Mr Mycroft persuade Jason to help with the bunting?' I said.

'With cash of course. He was rained off before he finished last night so he was pretty desperate, and Jason's too mean to help anyone for free. Why do they have bunting anyway? I thought this affair was deadly serious.'

'I suppose it's become a bit of a festival over the years. It's only people like Joseph and Sid that take it so seriously.'

'Watch out,' said Rib. 'Here comes Mr Critchley.'

He glided over to Rib's parents like a vampire about to overpower his prey.

'I trust this little picnic will be over by 1.50 p.m.,' he said smoothly. 'The band will proceed to the shed then, in order to start the parade at 2.00 p.m. precisely. It is customary to have The Fox and Lady garden and car park clear of spectators at that time, in order to protect The Foxer's identity. The band will enter through the car park, closing the gate behind them, after which customers and spectators may congregate there to see the procession commence. Have I made myself clear?'

Rib's parents exchanged irritated glances.

'Thank you *so* much for reminding us,' said Mrs Goddard sarcastically. 'Now, if you will excuse us, we have some sausages to attend to.'

They went into their kitchen, but it wasn't that easy to shake off Mr Critchley.

'May I give you a word of advice about the charcoal?' he said, oiling his way after them.

Rib sniggered.

'Mum will be furious,' she whispered. 'He kept her on the phone for half an hour last night. He gave her all the details twice and insisted that she wrote them down. What's this band he was talking about?'

'They call themselves the Skelland Players,' I said. 'The leader is Mr Carpenter, from Holme Burton. He plays the accordion and Mr Critchley's wife plays the violin. You'll recognize her. She looks just like her husband, only shorter. Her father used to do it, but he's too doddery now. I think there's another violinist, and a chap from Newmansey plays the flute. They always have a few people playing percussion. Baz Baldwin had a go last year, but Jayne says he's backed out this year.'

'I expect he couldn't manage to play the triangle and walk at the same time,' said Rib.

Her parents emerged from the kitchen, looking even more harassed.

'Got rid of him, have you?' said Rib.

She hadn't noticed Mr Critchley behind them. He gave her a stare icy enough to freeze her blood and strode out of the garden.

'Are you girls going to stand there all morning?' said Mr Goddard, taking out his irritation on us.

'Yes, unless you tell us what we're meant to be doing,' said Rib rudely.

People began to drift into the pub from midday. Most of them took their hot dogs inside as there was a chilly wind and the garden seats still looked very damp. Rib and I stayed outside and helped Mrs Goddard serve. The smoke from the barbecue got in my eyes and made them sting.

'They ought to have this fiasco in the summer,' said Mrs Goddard irritably. 'The rain isn't going to hold off for long, by the looks of things.'

The sky above was dapple grey, but over towards Cumbermouth was a bank of heavy rain clouds.

'It never rains on Foxing Day,' I said.

'Rubbish,' said Rib. 'You can't tell us it's never rained on the third Saturday in September. It must have been going on for years.'

I grinned.

'I was only repeating what Joseph told me,' I said. 'I think it's wishful thinking on his part. He can't bear to see anything go wrong with it.'

Everything went smoothly at first. The food tasted good, and the drink soon made people cheerful. By 1.45 p.m. the garden and car park were clear. Some people crowded into the bars, and others of us overflowed out of the front doors and on to Lady Lane. Mr Critchley had been waiting on the corner of Elm Street and Lady Lane for some time, glancing officiously at his watch every few minutes.

At 1.50 p.m. precisely The Skelland Players rounded the corner into Lady Lane. They moved together in a tight knot, with Mr Critchley following on behind. At first we could only pick out the boom boom of the drum, then as they drew closer the melody became dominant. It was a strange swirling tune, short and repetitive, that I recognized from previous years. People inside and outside the pub began to clap in time with the drum.

'What on earth are they wearing?' said Rib, as The Players drew nearer.

Men and women players alike wore red breeches, white shirts, black capes and sturdy black shoes.

'It's their traditional uniform,' I said. 'See the one in the middle with the hood? That's The Foxer. He always has the hood right over his head so nobody knows his identity.'

'The players are all crowding round him,' said Rib.

'That's the whole idea,' I said.

'It must be pretty easy to work out who it is,' said Rib. 'Just see who's missing from the crowd.'

'If people think they know,' I said, 'they keep it to themselves. Otherwise the ceremony doesn't work and The Foxer might be in danger.'

'You don't believe in all that do you?' said Rib.

'Of course not,' I said. 'It's just a bit of fun.'

'Well, at least we know it's not Critchley,' she said.

As soon as The Players had gone into the garden, people began to gather in the car park. Nick and Dean had propped their bikes against the pub garden wall and were attempting to peep over it by standing on the saddles. Mr Mycroft good-naturedly persuaded them to climb down. I couldn't see Sharlene anywhere, but she had probably stayed at home to add another layer to her nail varnish. Cherinea Johnson was there with her grandparents, and Baz and Jayne Baldwin stood primly, in matching blue anoraks, at the back of the crowd. As we walked towards the garden gate Rib spotted Sid and Nora Hambly.

'Oh no,' she said. 'They're coming over. Can't we run for it?'

'They're pretty harmless,' I said.

'Hello,' said Sid. 'Seen Joseph have you?'

'He was sitting in the bar a while ago,' said Rib. 'He looks awful. He told my Dad he was convinced something evil would happen today.'

'Let's hope today will undo the damage done when the box was tampered with,' said Sid.

'It's a bit parky,' said Nora. 'I hope it doesn't take them too long. Spot will catch a chill.'

She held the poor dog under her arm. He was wearing a ridiculous tartan coat. I could feel Rib wanting to laugh and tried not to look at her. Luckily the band started up again and people crowded towards the garden gate to wait for The Foxer to emerge.

He sprang out suddenly, in a billow of black. People gasped and drew back and a toddler screamed. The Fox's face leered, and his eyes saw everyone. The music pulsed louder now and The Foxer darted from side to side as he led the way out of the car park. People smiled and followed, embarrassed that for a moment they had felt fear.

The procession traditionally had three main stopping points, one where Elm Street joined the Cumbermouth Road, one at the northern boundary where Skelland met Holme Burton and a final one down Lady Lane, near the river's edge. Only a fraction of the villagers would follow the whole event, especially as the weather was so damp and blustery.

As we passed the front of the pub, thunder rumbled in the distance. Jason emerged and handed Rib a jacket.

'Mum says you're not to go with the procession unless you wear this,' he said. 'She says otherwise you'll catch your death of cold.'

Rib took it reluctantly.

'Where have *you* been?' she said. 'You've missed the start.'

'I had to get my camera ready,' he said. 'A set of pictures of Foxing Day would be great for my Drama Project, especially the ones I took from my bedroom window.'

'Jason!' said Rib indignantly. 'You've been spying.'

'Keep your voice down,' he said, grinning. 'We don't want to upset the old fogeys.'

'You know who The Foxer is, don't you?' said Rib.

Jason looked smug.

'Sorry girls,' he said. 'I must get up to the front of the procession if I'm to get any decent pictures.'

'Well, he might have let us in on it,' said Rib crossly.

'Hello girls,' said Joseph breathlessly, from behind us. 'Can an old man and his dog join you?'

We weren't sure whether he had heard Jason or not.

The rain didn't start until the second stop. By then only about fifteen followers remained. Jayne and Baz had sidled off as the procession passed through the village, murmuring something about homework, Cherinea had taken her grandparents home, and although Nick and Dean had cycled as far as the second stop, they had pedalled off at the first whiff of rain. Apart from the three of us, the remaining stalwarts were adults. They stood in a damp semicircle to watch the bounding Foxer, who seemed to have endless energy. As the tune played on and on they reached into bags for umbrellas and rain hats. Sid thoughtfully held an umbrella over Mrs Critchley's violin, leaving Nora to cope with a plastic rain hat she'd found tucked in a corner of her handbag.

'Thank goodness little Spot has got his coat on,' she said.

Mr Critchley wore a smart black hat which seemed to repel the water from his gaunt features, whilst Joseph, for once capless, refused to acknowledge the rain, letting it run down his forehead and drip off his eyebrows into his eyes. Rib's hair still stood up in greasy spikes, each with a drop of water at the end, like baubles on a Christmas tree.

'This is great,' she said. 'I love to get soaked.'

'You always were peculiar,' said Jason. He tucked his camera inside his anorak. 'I'll never get any decent pictures in this weather.'

'Look at Barker,' said Rib. 'He's soaking it up like a sponge. Joseph will have to squeeze him out when he gets home.'

I kept quiet. The rain dripped down my neck and seeped into my shoes.

'To Lady Lane!' said Mr Carpenter. 'And for heaven's sake somebody hold an umbrella over my accordion.'

So the bedraggled company walked back towards the village, losing still more people as it passed Rowan Street. The bunting along Elm Street hung limply down, as a reminder of the festival there should have been, and a toddler waved from behind a steamy window.

It was half way down Lady Lane that we noticed something peculiar.

'It's stopped,' said Sid.

'The road's dry,' said Rib, whose hair was sagging a little like a droopy crown. 'It hasn't rained here.'

'Praise be,' said Joseph. 'This might save the day.'

Umbrellas went down, Barker shook himself and a new bounce went into the steps of the Skelland Players. And all the time, The Foxer pranced and danced towards the final stop, flapping the soaking black cloth around his nimble body.

We walked past the building site and Joseph's cottage to the end of Lady Lane. The Skelland Players stood at the bottom of the dyke, facing the tiny audience. The Foxer danced on in front of them. Jason got out his camera, Mr Critchley adjusted his hat and Nora anxiously dabbed at Spot's head with a paper hanky.

'She'll wipe the spot off if she's not careful,' whispered Rib.

Barker gave himself another good shake and looked anxiously up at his unhappy master, while the crowd began to clap.

'This is more like it,' said Sid.

The ritual always ended with The Foxer running up the dyke to repel evil from the very edge of Skelland.

'Up the dyke,' yelled someone.

The music grew louder as The Foxer obeyed. He stood at the top of the dyke, towering above us, with his arms outstretched beneath the sodden cloth.

That should have been the end of it. Cheers were ready on our lips, but the events that followed silenced them. As The Foxer stood there, black against a white sky, a jagged streak of lightning seemed to split the sky in two behind him. In the clap of thunder that followed, The Foxer seemed to lose his balance, tottered back a few steps and fell screaming down the dyke towards the river.

The music stopped and for a second nobody moved.

'Somebody get him out!' said Nora. 'The evil's back. He'll be drowned.'

Still nobody moved. Barker growled. Then Sid found the strength to run up the bank.

'Can you see him?' shouted someone.

Sid stood still, gazing down in horror.

'Do something man,' cried Mr Critchley.

'Come on,' said Rib. 'He's going to let the chap drown.'

We ran up the bank, the cool air catching in our throats. Rib got there first. I looked over her shoulder. In the muddy water, a little way out, something black was sliding under the surface. But Rib was pointing at the mud beneath us, where something moved. It was a woman, dressed in white. Her scrabbling hands grasped the grasses on the edge of the dyke to pull herself slowly upwards. Once off the mud, she stood. Slime stuck to her face and caked her long hair. Her dress clung around her body weighing her down as she tried to climb up the bank.

Rib screamed. This seemed to bring Sid to his senses. He turned and ran down towards the crowd. I followed, pulling Rib with me.

'The Foxer's drowned,' he said. His voice was taut and anguished. 'The Lady's back. She's climbing out of the river.'

As the crowd watched, the muddied figure staggered up on to the dyke.

'Run for it!' cried Sid.

Most people began to run up the lane, musicians and audience alike. Someone dropped a tambourine and a black umbrella lay half open, flapping a little like an injured bat. Joseph stood quite still, making a strange moaning sound, and Mr Critchley and Mr Carpenter waited silently by his side. Jason was adjusting his camera as if nothing was amiss and behind him stood Mr Mycroft. Rib tugged my arm urgently.

'Come on,' she said. 'Let's get out of here!'

Then Mr Mycroft spoke.

'Angela,' he said. 'It's my Angela.'

Chapter Eleven

Half an hour later we were sitting drinking tea at Joseph's cottage. Angela Mycroft, her face washed, sat in the armchair, wrapped in a huge towel. Clive was beside her, with a protective arm around her shoulder. Sid and Nora sat stiffly at the table, Rib and Jason sat on the floor with me and Joseph perched on the little stool. All eyes were focused upon Angela, who hadn't spoken since emerging from the river.

'You should never have allowed me to do it,' she said, looking at Joseph.

'You knew?' said Sid.

Joseph nodded miserably.

'What else could we do?' he said. 'No one came forward this year. We decided that someone on the committee would have to do it. We couldn't spare Bill Carpenter. There wouldn't be a band if he didn't cajole them into coming. Den Critchley felt the arrangements would fall through if he weren't seen to be present and I thought my legs wouldn't be up to it. I was afraid of ruining everything.'

'We kept hoping someone would contact us, right until Wednesday,' said Angela.

'That was the night you saw the ghost,' said Jason cheerfully.

'Aye, lad. We realized a decision would have to be made. We held a meeting at Critchley's place.'

'Joseph felt that to *ask* someone to take it on would cause trouble. He was frightened after what he'd seen that night,' said Angela. 'There was never any suggestion that it had to be a man so *I* volunteered.'

Clive squeezed her shoulders proudly.

'Whatever did old Critchley have to say about that?' said Rib.

'There wasn't much he *could* say,' said Angela. 'He'd already spent ten minutes telling us how indispensable he was for crowd control.'

'But he didn't like it,' said Joseph. 'And, no offence to Angela, but neither did I. I knew it would mean trouble.'

'What about Bill?' I said.

'He backed me up,' said Angela. 'And I was really pleased with myself. I'd no idea what effect that awful costume would have on me. I know it sounds silly, but it seemed to take over. It made me run and leap until

I'd not an ounce of energy left. I'd worn this nightie underneath because it was such a cold day, but the heat in there was unbearable. I thought I was finished when I fell off the dyke. I don't know how I found the energy to get the costume off. I'm sorry it went in the water, but at the time it felt as though it was it or me.'

Jason looked uncomfortably pink and Rib looked dangerously as if she was going to mention the Spooky Dress affair.

'Do you think Critchley and Bill have caught up with the others?' I said.

'I hope so, lass,' said Sid gravely. 'Things are bad enough as it is. We don't want them telling people The Foxer is drowned and that The Lady's been seen in daylight. They must be told it was all a misunderstanding, but the less said about the lost costume the better.'

'They were so terrified they've probably reached Cumbermouth by now,' said Jason gleefully. 'It'll be front page news.'

'It would be a great help to us all if you took things more seriously, young man,' said Nora sniffily. 'We all saw you, taking pictures as if you were on a Sunday School outing. Some people can be in a place for a couple of weeks and think they own it.'

'And some people can move out of a place and think *they* still own it,' said Rib.

'Let's not get heated,' said Mr Mycroft. 'I agree with Sid, the less said the better. The committee can meet in due course to decide what's to be done, but now I'd appreciate it if Mr Hambly would drive Angela and me home.'

'We are the only ones who know what poor Angela suffered and that the costume is lost. I'm sure none of the adults would dream of blabbing, but can we trust these children to keep *their* mouths shut?' said Nora.

'We don't want half the children from Stansholme Middle to turn up looking for ghosts.'

'Of course you can trust us,' said Rib hotly. 'But what if my parents notice that the costume has not been returned?'

'Whether anything's said or not, the harm's been done,' said Joseph. 'I saw The Lady after the costume was tampered with. What are we to expect now the costume is at the bottom of the river?'

'It may turn up somewhere,' I said. 'Would you like us to go and have another look?'

'I looked up and down river before we left,' said Sid. 'It's sunk without trace.'

'You'd think it would float, wouldn't you?' said Rib. 'Perhaps it will come up to the surface again.'

'It's gone for sure,' said Joseph. 'And I'll not rest easy in my bed tonight.'

'Why not stay with us tonight,' said Angela Mycroft kindly. 'You could come with us now. I'm sure the Hamblys won't mind squeezing another person in their van. I know Clive is worried about me, but there's nothing a good night's sleep won't cure.'

'Thanks lass,' said Joseph. 'But I think it best if I stay here and face whatever comes.'

Chapter Twelve

The first burglary happened on Monday.

'Heard about the mysterious theft in Holme Burton?' said Rib, at morning break on Wednesday.

'Yes, Dad spotted it in the paper last night. They gave it two lines on the back page.'

'Did you see what was taken?' she said.

'Only an emerald brooch.'

'Exactly,' she said. '*And* there was no sign of a break-in.'

'How do you know?'

'I just happened to notice Nora and Sid Hambly having an important-looking conversation with Joseph in the car park last night. He was on his way home, but they seemed to want to talk to him pretty urgently.'

'So you listened in?'

'There's no law against standing by our own garden gate. I couldn't help it if they wanted to have a secret discussion on the other side. Anyway I don't know why you're looking so shocked. I bet you can't wait to hear what they said.'

'I know I'm going to hear it anyway,' I laughed. 'You look as if you're about to burst.'

'Nora knew all about the theft,' said Rib. 'She was really proud of herself because the police had questioned her. She cleans the Carpenters' house on Monday afternoons. They live next door to the house that was burgled and the police hoped she might have seen somebody skulking about. Not that they seemed to be taking it that seriously. The woman who owned it was a bit absent-minded according to them. They'd had to break into her house the other week when she'd locked herself out. She told the police she'd taken the brooch out of the safe ready for the Carpenters' dinner party that night but when she went to put it on she couldn't find it anywhere. As far as they knew she had been in the house all day apart from when she popped round for a cup of tea with Mrs Carpenter.'

'And could Nora tell them anything?'

'She was able to confirm the cup of tea story. She, Mrs Carpenter and the woman from next door had all had a break together. She said it couldn't have taken more than fifteen minutes. It was what she had seen later that worried her, and even though it might stir up a lot of trouble she'd felt honour bound to tell them.'

'Whatever do you mean?'

'She stayed until the evening that day to help Mrs Carpenter to prepare for the dinner party and she swears that she saw a fox in the next door's garden.'

'You're joking?'

'I'm not,' said Rib. 'And then the police turned up. It frightened the wits out of her.'

'The police told her not to worry about a fox because they'd never known one to attack anyone so she explained that, for a moment, she had believed that The Fox of Skelland was back, but that she realized it was rather silly of her to believe in such nonsense.'

'They'll just think she's mad,' I said.

'That's what she hoped. She felt she ought to let Joseph know, rather than him hear of it from elsewhere.'

'Who else has she told then?'

'Nobody. I think she was afraid the police might notice fox prints in the woman's garden and start a Fox of Skelland hunt. They did a routine check of her bag before Sid came to collect her and the bike, but she said they seemed more interested in the cup of tea and biscuits Mrs Carpenter was handing round.'

'What did poor Joseph make of it?'

'He went into his "I told you it would end in tears" routine and said that if the police did take her seriously he would feel it his duty to tell them that he had seen The Lady. And in addition to that, he swears that Barker kicked up a fuss on the night of the burglary, but that he had not dared to open his curtains. Nora said perhaps he should look out next time.'

'The police are not going to take The Fox business seriously unless they live in Skelland.'

'What difference does it make where they live?'

'If they lived in Skelland they'd know that a fox has never been seen in the village or surroundings since they started Foxing Day all those years ago.'

'That sounds like another of Joseph's "It never rains on Foxing Day" fantasies,' said Rib. 'I thought foxes were commonplace everywhere now. There must have been *some*.'

'Not as far as anybody knows. Not until last Friday night anyway.'

'What's so special about last Friday?'

'That's when *I* saw one.'

'*You* saw one?'

'I think I was half asleep, but I thought I saw it running down Elm Street in the rain storm, with its head held high and its tail as bushy as if it were dry.'

'Either there have always been foxes or you have been seeing things,' said Rib. 'Unless, of course, The Fox of Skelland *is* back.'

Chapter Thirteen

It was Rib's idea to have me to stay. She sprang it on me on the way home.

'I've asked Mum if you can stay the night so we can plan our Drama for tomorrow.'

'What Drama?'

'She says if your Mum agrees, it's all right with her. You can collect your stuff and come straight round for tea.'

It wasn't until we went up to Jason's room after tea that she revealed the real reason behind the invitation.

'Jason is beginning to think that there might be something in this Fox and Lady business, aren't you Jace?'

He looked a bit embarrassed.

'He thought it was very strange that Angela Mycroft felt as if the costume had "taken over" when she was wearing it. Jason only wore the bottom part, but we saw how odd it made him feel. It even affected us. Remember how fox-like his mask looked when he was spinning around?'

'That was probably a trick of the light,' said Jason. 'But I definitely felt peculiar when I was dancing, and you've got to admit it's a bit odd that since the Fox costume was tampered with The Lady has been spotted *and* Foxing Day went wrong.'

'He's always liked mysteries,' said Rib. 'It's best to go along with him.'

'I'd have thought it was all coincidence if there hadn't been the stolen jewellery incident,' said Jason. 'It all fits with Joseph's story of The Lady's fox. There was no trace of a break-in on Monday and Nora saw a fox in the area for the first time since The Lady was chased out of Skelland.'

'Not *quite* the first time,' said Rib gleefully. 'Tell him Sam.'

I told him I thought I'd seen a fox on Friday night. It seemed to strengthen his interest.

'So tell her what we are going to do, Jason,' said Rib.

'We're going to the scene of the first sighting.'

He paused for effect.

'After dark.'

'Isn't it exciting?' said Rib.

'Not very,' I said. 'It's freezing out there. And besides, what are your parents going to think about us going out at night?'

'We'll have Jason to protect us. He's not as tough as me, but he looks bigger,' said Rib. 'Anyway, they may *forget* we're going. That way they won't be worried.'

'You mean you have no intention of telling them?'

'Exactly,' she said.

We were just tiptoeing down the stairs when we heard

sounds of excitement from the kitchen. We stopped above the curve in the stairs to listen. Joseph's voice came from the kitchen.

'It's true,' he wailed. 'She's back. I've seen her again. I shouldn't be telling you, but I didn't think my legs would get me to Den Critchley's house. I feel bad enough that I mentioned it in front of everyone the other day, but fear can do funny things to a chap's discretion.'

'Calm down, old chap,' said Mr Goddard. 'What happened the other night is yesterday's news. A man was celebrating a Pools win last night. He bought drinks for everyone, as many as they wanted. That should have put all thoughts of ghosts out of their heads. I should sit down and tell us exactly what you saw. Your secret's safe with us.'

'You're very kind,' said Joseph. 'I've had a nasty shock.'

'I'd better get back to the bar,' said Mrs Goddard.

'Get him a whisky, Mary,' called Mr Goddard. 'And give our friend Critchley a ring will you?'

'Joseph only does it for the free booze,' laughed Rib. 'I bet Dad wishes he *had* announced it in the bar. A ghost sighting would be good for custom.'

'Not as good as that Pools winner,' said Jason.

'I'd not have looked out had it not been for Barker howling,' said Joseph. 'I've not dared to look out of my window after dark since I first saw Her. I shut my curtains again tonight, but he made such a fuss I knew he'd not calm down until I investigated.'

I peeped over the banister and saw Mrs Goddard bustling across the hall with the drink.

'I can see the river from my hobby room,' said Joseph. 'And when I looked over there I saw Her again. She was on the dyke, all in white. Then she walked down, as if she were climbing into a boat, and floated across the river. She seemed to glow as she went across. Then she disappeared ... she must have gone down before she reached the other side. It was drizzling but I could see enough.'

'It sounds just like the last time,' said Mr Goddard. 'Did you notice anything else?'

'I did,' said Joseph. 'And I didn't like it at all ... there was an animal at her feet. She lifted it up under her arm before she went down the dyke.'

'What sort of animal?' asked Mr Goddard.

'A fox,' said Joseph. His voiced trembled. 'I've seen The Fox, Mr Goddard, The Fox of Skelland.'

Ten minutes later we were walking down Lady Lane.

'It's a good job Joseph had to take Barker out,' said Jason. 'Otherwise we'd never have got past them.'

'Why are we doing this?' I said, as we walked down the dark lane. 'Wouldn't it have been better to wait until Critchley and Co. arrived?'

'Do you really think they'd want three children tagging along?' said Jason. 'They'll be so agitated they'll want to make sure nobody hears of it. They see their job as protecting the other villagers from evil, and that includes unnecessary worry.'

'It's not worrying us,' I said, 'so why should anyone else be bothered?'

'It is a bit creepy down here,' said Rib.

We each held a torch, but they became less and less effective as we walked further away from the pub lights.

'You wouldn't think twice about walking down here in daylight,' said Jason.

'What if we see Her?' I said. I was beginning to feel nervous, especially as Rib had gone uncharacteristically quiet.

'It depends how frequently she appears,' said Jason,

as if he went ghost hunting every night. 'She's been once tonight if Joseph is to be believed.'

'I hope it won't take long,' said Rib. 'It's drizzling again.'

We passed the building site, our shoes slithering a little on the muddy tracks. Further down the lane was Joseph's cottage. He had forgotten to turn out his hobby room lights or close his curtains.

'I'll just make sure he's locked up,' I said. The metal gate scraped across the concrete path as I entered the garden. A chicken clucked disapprovingly from the hen coop and the rain rattled on an upturned bucket. It was reassuring to find the cottage door firmly locked.

'Whose bright idea was it to come out without umbrellas?' said Rib.

I scraped the gate shut.

'Let's go back,' said Rib. 'I'm drenched.'

'I thought you liked getting wet,' I said.

'We may as well finish the job now we've got this far,' said Jason.

The grass on the dyke was slippery. It was quite dizzying to stand on the top and hear the river sliding along below. The lights of Thorncoates shone dimly through the rain.

'Let's stay where we are,' said Jason. 'We don't want to scare Her off.'

We shone our torches around our feet.

'Someone else has been along here,' said Jason.

There were several footprints, some of them our own.

'There are always prints along here,' I said. 'Lots of people walk along the top.'

'But how many people go down the mud to the river,' said Rib.

She was directing her torch down towards the water.

'There are some marks in the mud,' she said. 'Shine your torches where mine is pointing.'

'Footprints!' said Jason. 'But they've sunk too deep to see any detail. And they're full of rain. It's impossible to tell if they are male or female.'

'And *look* near the water,' said Rib.

There was a huge gouge in the mud as if something had been dragged on to it, and snaking its way up beside the footprints was the imprint of a rope. Water streamed down it towards the river.

'Someone has had a boat here,' said Jason. He shone his torch toward a knobbly rock on the dyke. 'And I bet that's what it was moored to.'

'Look!' said Rib, pointing her torch towards the footprints again.

At the top of the mud bank was another set of prints. Each full of water, they winked in the torchlight like cat's eyes. They were animal prints, such as those of a dog or cat, and followed the human prints a little way down before disappearing completely.

'An animal about the size of a fox,' said Jason. 'It made some prints before it was picked up . . .'

We walked back to the pub. We were too drenched to worry about more rain. None of us spoke until we were nearing the building site.

'It's a pity,' said Jason. 'I rather liked the idea of the ghost.'

'Me too,' said Rib. 'But those were real tracks made by a real person.'

There was relief in her voice.

'Yes,' I said. 'But why would anybody go to all that trouble to frighten Joseph? I thought *everybody* liked him.'

'Apparently not,' said Jason.

As we passed the building site we saw a car pull out of the pub car park.

'It's coming down here!' said Rib. 'Torches out everyone.'

'They'll see us in the headlights,' I said.

'Quick!' said Jason. 'In here.'

We hid behind a pile of bricks until the car had passed.

'It must be Den Critchley taking Joseph home,' I said.

'I'm surprised he dares to go back after what he saw,' said Jason.

'If he *did* see anything,' said Rib.

'Whatever do you mean?' said Jason. 'We know it wasn't The Fox and Lady, but we all saw the tracks.'

'Someone was there all right,' I said.

'Perhaps it was Joseph,' said Rib. 'He might have put the tracks there himself. He's got Barker to use for fake Fox prints.'

'Why would he want anybody to think The Fox and Lady were back?' said Jason.

'To take their attention away from something else?' said Rib.

'Not Joseph,' I said. 'He wouldn't do a thing like that.'

Chapter Fourteen

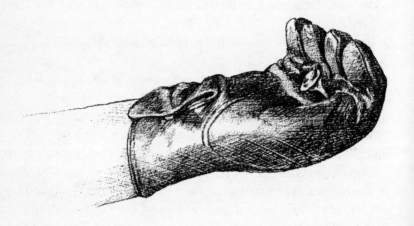

Neither Mr nor Mrs Goddard was in the kitchen when we got back, so we managed to get up the stairs without being seen.

'We'll come to your room when we've dried out a bit,' said Rib to Jason. She got towels out of the airing cupboard on the way to her room.

'I hope you brought some spare clothes,' she said.

She took off her jacket, sweater, shoes and jeans and rubbed her hair with a towel.

'I've only got clean undies and socks,' I said, 'but I can't turn up for school in those tomorrow. I wish you'd warned me to get changed before I came.'

I kicked off my school shoes and peeled off my socks. They had dark black stains where the shoe polish had soaked in.

'I'll have to do something about these,' I said. 'My mother will go spare if she sees them like this.'

'You can rub them with some soap in the bathroom,' said Rib. 'And we'll see if we can get them dry on the radiator.'

My school blouse was dry, but my anorak and skirt were drenched. I wouldn't have minded so much if the rain had got rid of the gravy stain on my skirt, but it seemed to make it more noticeable if anything.

Mrs Goddard called up the stairs.

'Rib, there's an Isabelle Podd on the phone for you.'

'Quick, find me some clothes,' said Rib.

I pulled at a sleeve that stuck out from under her bed. It was her sloppy sweatshirt. It came out complete with under-bed fluff, but at least it was dry.

'Coming,' she called, pulling the sweatshirt over her head.

She slipped on some ridiculous fluffy pink slippers and slopped down the stairs.

Rib was looking very pleased with herself when she returned. I was still trying to get the tangles out of my hair.

'Whatever did *she* want,' I said crossly.

'Her aunt lives in one of the posh houses in Holme Burton. She was letting me know that there has been another strange burglary there. Someone's diamond ring has disappeared.'

'You've told her? I thought it had been agreed that it was better to keep this business to ourselves. Nora Hambly was right. You think you own the place.'

I began to throw my wet clothes into my bag.

'What *are* you doing?' said Rib.

'I'm going home,' I shouted. 'I should never have agreed to come in the first place. You treat the whole business like some sort of joke, you tamper with things that don't belong to you and *then* have the nerve to suggest that Joseph Jenkins is a liar.'

Rib looked irritatingly calm.

'Don't you think your parents will be a little bit surprised if you turn up without your skirt on?' she said.

I couldn't help smiling.

'Why not hear my explanation while you wait for your skirt to dry,' she said, grinning. 'Put your fancy dressing gown on and we'll go to Jason's room.'

Jason was almost as annoyed with Rib as I was.

'You asked *her*?' he said. 'She's poisonous. Have you seen Winston when she's around? I've never seen that guy frightened before. She'll never keep The Fox story secret.'

'As it happens,' said Rib, 'I didn't tell her anything about The Fox, or The Lady for that matter. She was boasting at school, saying that one of the houses near her aunt's place in Holme Burton had been burgled. She said it was a constant worry for her aunt as they had so many things worth stealing, but she didn't suppose it was something *we* had to worry about.

'I said no burglar would ever go back to Holme Burton now they'd heard there was nothing worth pinching. She was so annoyed that I knew she'd let me know if she heard anything else.'

'Were you *expecting* more thefts?' said Jason.

'Yes,' she said, 'especially when I heard Joseph had seen The Fox.'

'You think he's using The Fox and Lady as a cover,' said Jason.

She nodded

'What rubbish,' I said. 'If Joseph was stealing from Holme Burton he'd hardly want to draw attention to himself. He'd find it hard to get there too. He's only got an old bike and last time I saw it the tyres were split.'

'He could take Barker for walkies across the fields,' said Rib.

'In which case he'd have been seen,' I said. 'Have the police got any *intelligent* theories, or didn't Isabelle tell you that?'

'She said they were baffled. Only two precious pieces of jewellery were taken and the thief left no clues. They've questioned people in the area but nobody saw anything suspicious.'

We heard voices in the hall.

'Have a listen,' said Jason. 'Perhaps Critchley and Co. are back.'

Rib stuck her tousled head out of the door.

'It's Sid and Nora,' she said. 'Let's go down for a cup of tea and find out what they're up to.'

Sid stood by the back door, peering out at the rain. Nora sat primly at the kitchen table. Her face was nervous, and yet slightly excited, at the prospect of revealing some good gossip. Spot snuffled around under the table in search of crumbs.

'Oh it's you,' she said, when we entered. 'We're waiting to speak to Mr Goddard.'

'Dad says he'll be a while,' lied Rib. 'Can *we* help?'

'We were looking for Joseph,' said Sid.

Nora gave him a warning look.

'There's no harm in telling them,' said Sid. 'They saw what happened on Foxing Day.'

'And we *have* kept quiet about it,' said Rib smiling sickeningly.

'I hardly dare talk about it,' said Nora, her lip trembling. 'Your father says Joseph saw The Lady tonight, and The Fox was with her.'

'Really?' said Rib. 'He must have been very upset. What do you think it all means?'

'It means trouble,' said Nora, her lip trembling. 'Did you hear about the burglary at Holme Burton?'

'Yes,' said Rib. 'A friend said her aunt's neighbour had lost a precious brooch on Monday.'

'"Lost" doesn't come into it,' said Nora. 'I was working over there on Monday, next door to the house . . . and I saw The Fox.'

'*You* did?' said Jason. 'It *must* be back then. How does it get the stuff out?'

'Nobody knows,' said Nora.

'It's a mystery, just as it was all those years ago,' said Sid. 'And now there's been another theft.'

'At Holme Burton?' I said.

'Yes, a diamond ring went missing. And to think I'd been at the very house.'

He shivered.

'I could have run into The Fox. Mrs Carpenter had asked me to advise a friend about her guttering. We're working right opposite her house. I went there during my lunchbreak to have a look. It was only a cleaning job, so I sent a couple of the lads over. By the time I was locking up the enclosure this evening I saw the police there. I went over, of course, but there wasn't much I could tell them. Nobody in the area had seen a thing. They thought it might be one of the lads on the site. They'd all left by then, including the two who did the gutters, but the officers still had a snoop around. They found nothing of course. The lads are an honest bunch.'

'It was The Fox,' said Nora. 'We came to warn Joseph that he might see it again but we were too late. The poor fellow has already seen it. He must have been terrified.'

'It's not done *you* much good either, dear,' said Sid, putting a protective arm round her. 'She's had to give in her notice a bit earlier than we thought, you know. The whole thing has been bad for her nerves.'

'I've told Mrs Carpenter I'll do for her next Monday.

She's got her family coming and wants the house spick and span. She asked me to stay late to do some baking for the freezer and I couldn't refuse, but apart from that I'll stay at home in Thorncoates.'

Later I lay in Rib's room. The Put-U-Up was very uncomfortable and car headlights shone brightly through unlined curtains as people drove out of the car park. I thought over the events of the last few days. Everything had changed. I thought about Joseph. I had always felt secure with him, trusted him.

Soon I felt myself drifting into sleep.

... Time can't stand still ... A dog needs a sense of achievement ... some say he's sinister, but he keeps the evil away ...

'I've been thinking,' said Rib dreamily.
'What about?' I said struggling out of slumber for a second.
'Pipes ...'

Chapter Fifteen

'There's your friend on the phone for you,' said Mum on Friday evening.

For a moment I thought she meant Emma and was surprised at how nervous I felt. So much had changed since she left.

'It's me,' said Rib. 'If I put the phone down quickly it's because Mum is about.'

I didn't feel like talking to her. She and Jason had been off school with a stomach bug since our ghost-hunting and I'd had to face school alone wearing a skirt that had moulded itself into the curves of one of their radiators. In addition to that I had failed to rub the black marks off my socks before my mother got hold of them. I had not been allowed to visit the invalids, partly because Mum didn't want *me* to be sick all over the place and partly because she suspected that Rib had something to do with my ruined socks and skirt.

'Sorry about the other night,' said Rib.

'So am I,' I said coldly.

'I hope you managed to get your socks clean . . . I expect your skirt hung out a bit during the day . . . didn't it? . . . Listen, I've been doing a bit of research . . .'

'You're *meant* to be ill,' I said crossly.

'I was feeling a bit better this lunchtime,' she said. 'And I just happened to get talking to some chaps from the building site. They were at the bar.'

'I thought your parents preferred you to keep out of there.'

'I wasn't exactly "in". I just leant through the hall door a bit. I wanted to ask them about the pipes.'

'What pipes?'

'You remember. The yellow sausages we saw from that house. There was a hideous trench with fences on either side, coming across from Holme Burton. The bit they fence off is called the "easement".'

'How fascinating,' I said sarcastically.

'The blokes were telling me that Sid's lot have laid pipes beside the trench nearly all the way across from Holme Burton now. They put them on piles of wood called "skids" and weld them all together before any of them are sunk in the trench.'

'So?'

'A couple more days and they'll lower them in. They're flexible enough to be lowered in a few at a time without the whole lot coming apart. They said something about "side-booms" but I didn't really understand what they were talking about.'

'Have you called me away from my Maths homework to tell me *this*?' I said.

'I haven't told you the really interesting bit yet.'

She lowered her voice so that I had to strain to hear what she was saying.

'I asked them if I could get along the pipes. They said they doubted it because they only have a diameter of about 12 inches. That must be about 30 centimetres.'

'Why do you *want* to go along?' I said.

'I don't,' she said. 'But it might be possible to train a dog to do it, especially a clever one like Barker. Do you see what I'm getting at?'

I did.

'Why don't you leave Barker and Joseph alone,' I said. 'Any little dog, clever *or* stupid, could go along them, but have you ever heard of one that could nip into someone's home, take a brooch from their dressing table and creep out again without being seen?'

'Barker is pretty amazing,' she said.

'He must be,' I said. 'If he is the culprit, and assuming he let Joseph in on the secret, what has Joseph done with the loot?'

'He's taken it across the river,' she said. 'Come with me and Jace tomorrow morning and I should be able to prove it. I'll see you at about ten o'clock. Bring your bike ... we've got a bit of a journey ... oh, and I shouldn't wear your school skirt if I was you.'

She put down the phone before I had time to argue.

Chapter Sixteen

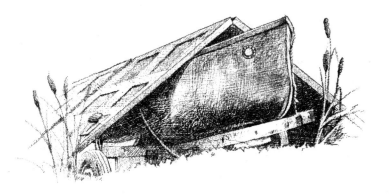

I was surprised to see how pale Rib looked the following morning.

'You will make sure Rebecca doesn't overdo things won't you Samantha?' said Mrs Goddard. 'It's been a nasty bug. I'm not very keen on her cycling, but it isn't far to your house. Jason wanted to take you up on your invitation, but he really ought to stay in bed for another day.'

'I'll be fine,' said Rib. 'Won't I, Sam?'

'Is it far to Thorncoates?' she said as we cycled down Elm Street.

'Don't you know?'

'I've seen it over the river. It looks pretty close.'

'I know it *looks* close,' I said, 'but we have to go down to Newmansey to get across.'

We passed my house, and the Kilbys' next door. Nick and Dean were slouching about in their front garden.

'Where are you going?' said Dean.

'Stansholme,' said Rib. 'Isabelle Podd has asked us round for coffee.'

Lies came very easily to her.

'Want to join us?'

'Not if you paid us,' said Nick. 'I'd rather do my homework than see *her*.'

'Where does your mother think we're going?' I said as we pedalled down the Cumbermouth Road. 'I don't expect you told her you were going to Thorncoates to prove that Joseph Jenkins is a thief.'

'She thinks your mother is taking us shopping in Cumbermouth.'

'What if she bumps into Mum in Skelland? It will look as if *I* have been lying.'

Rib shrugged.

'I'll think of something,' she said.

We soon turned off for Newmansey. The road was single track with lots of bends and was lined on either side with pretty hedgerows. A rabbit zigzagged across the road in front of us and birds twittered cheerfully. I began to relax a little.

'This is awful,' said Rib, breathlessly. 'Is it much further?'

She seemed to be slowing down, even though her bike was far superior to mine.

'We're only half way there,' I said with satisfaction. 'Don't forget *you* were the one who wanted to come.'

Once over the bridge we joined a busy road. Here conversation was out of the question. I let Rib go in front. Large lorries roared past us, filling the air with choking fumes and a car driver beeped when Rib swerved out to avoid a pot-hole.

I was relieved to turn off for Thorncoates.

'How do we get to the river?' said Rib.

'Turn right somewhere, I expect.'

We rode between terraces of thin red-bricked houses, where lines of drab washing hung. A dirty-faced toddler stared at us over his garden gate and a balding cat sat on the dusty pavement scratching at his fleas.

The centre of Thorncoates was equally uninspiring, with a few scruffy shops and an ugly garage.

'Let's get a drink,' said Rib. 'I'm parched.'

We propped our bikes outside a little serve-yourself called Buywell. Rib flopped down on to the pavement and scratched around the grime with a filthy lolly stick. Her pale face was dotted with beads of perspiration.

'Do you think they've heard of Coke here?' she said, doubtfully.

'Probably not,' I laughed. It was hard to be cross with her for long. 'What an awful place this is. There aren't any trees. The way Sid and Nora were talking I thought it would look like Paradise. Their bungalow is on the outskirts somewhere. Perhaps it looks better there.'

'Haven't you been here before?'

'I bet nobody from Skelland has been here since they lost the little ferry boat.'

'They haven't missed much,' said Rib. 'No wonder The Lady didn't bother to get to the other side.'

Her voice sounded wobbly. She rested her head down on her knees.

'Are you all right?' I said.

'Just a bit dizzy,' she said. 'I was sick again this morning. I didn't tell Mum because I knew she wouldn't let me come.'

'I'll get the drinks,' I said.

'I was hoping you'd say that,' she said. 'I forgot to bring any money.'

We found the track to the river without much trouble.

It was a grassy lane that ran between allotments. We left our bikes at the top of the lane and walked towards the river. Weeds tangled their way over the fences on either side of the track. One or two of the plots were beautifully tended, but most had the same aura of neglect as the village centre, with their tumble-down sheds and waist-high weeds.

Soon we stood at the bottom of the dyke.

'Go steady,' said Rib. 'We don't want to be seen from the other side.'

'I suppose you think Joseph will be there with binoculars and shotgun,' I said.

'I don't know,' she said seriously, 'but I think we'd do better to climb up by those hawthorn bushes.'

We climbed up the dyke and peered through the branches. The track was nearly opposite the end of Lady Lane. It was strange to see a place I knew so well from the other side of the river.

'There's a pretty good view of Joseph's cottage,' said Rib. 'And look beyond it. There are the pipes. They'll reach the building site soon. It would be easy for Joseph to walk that far. He could send Barker off down the pipes to get the loot. He'd tell him to bring it back into the pipes and stay there until the men stop work. Then he'd wait until dark to get Barker out, dress up as The Lady and bring it across here to hide it.'

'The whole idea of a little dog understanding those instructions and baffling the police is ridiculous,' I said. 'And how do you think he got in and out of the pipes without any of the workmen noticing him?'

'Do you believe The Fox did it all those years ago?' she said.

'That was different.'

'It was very similar,' she said. 'People really believed The Fox was responsible and there weren't any pipes to hide in then.'

'Sid and Nora think it's back,' I said.

'And we owe it to them, and anybody else who is frightened, to find the truth,' said Rib. 'There are all sorts of possible explanations. Do you think Joseph and Barker have an accomplice? Perhaps they're in league with Isabelle's aunt.'

I shrugged. I didn't know what to think any more.

'I wonder where the boat is?' said Rib.

She found parallel wheel tracks on the grass that ran from the water's edge, over the dyke and down towards the allotments.

'This might lead us to it,' she said.

'Hasn't anybody told you that boats don't have wheels?' I said. 'Someone has wheeled an old pram into the river. People are always dumping junk in it.'

'I'm not so sure,' said Rib. 'If you look carefully you can see some old tracks too. The same thing has been wheeled over here several times.'

The tracks led to some weed-ridden allotments.

'They seem to have stopped,' said Rib. 'But they could have been wheeled through the weeds. It wouldn't be difficult to straighten up the weeds afterwards.'

She strode into the weeds and I followed. I got my leg caught in some brambles and was glad I had worn trousers. I almost hoped she *would* find a boat, then we could go home. Otherwise she might suggest diving in the river to see if it was hidden at the bottom.

'Look!' she said triumphantly, three allotments later. 'A boat.'

Almost hidden by brambles were two wooden garage doors, propped up together like a ridge tent and underneath them was a small boat.

'It's got a little motor,' said Rib. 'And look underneath. It's resting on some wheels.'

'Can we go home now?' I said, rubbing my arm where the brambles had drawn blood.

'We can't go without looking inside,' she said. 'Let's pull it out a bit.'

'Do you think we should?' I said. 'Someone might see us.'

'I doubt it,' said Rib. 'It doesn't look as if anybody has worked round here for a long time.'

I looked carefully around us. Apart from a spiral of smoke from a distant bonfire there was no sign of life.

'All right,' I said. 'But I'll do the pulling. I don't want you fainting all over the place.'

I pulled hard and managed to drag the boat out. Inside it was a sack, tied loosely at the top.

'The loot!' said Rib excitedly.

'Don't be ridiculous,' I said. 'You don't think anybody would leave some valuable jewellery in the middle of an allotment do you?'

She undid the bag carefully and tipped the contents into the bottom of the boat.

'A dirty old sheet and a lamp,' she said flatly.

I opened out the sheet. Something brown fell out . . . something furry, with a bushy tail.

'Ugh! A dead fox,' said Rib. 'Get rid of it!'

I picked it up. The stuffed fox head and tail were genuine, but they were fixed to some brown fur fabric. The material must have been a remnant. It still had a sticky price tag on the back.

'It's a fox costume,' I said. 'There is some Velcro along the sides.'

'I get it!' said Rib. 'It's a costume for Barker. The Velcro would fasten under his stomach and under his chin. What a brilliant idea!'

She picked up the sheet.

'And look at this,' she said. 'He's made it into a cloak. It's got a hood.'

'Pack it away,' I said. 'Let's get out of here.'

'Yes,' she said. 'We don't want him to catch us here. He said The Lady seemed to glow. I'd like to know how he managed that. Perhaps the lamp had something to do with it.' She switched on the lamp. 'It's pretty powerful. Perhaps he directed it at himself like a sort of spotlight.'

'And I suppose he leapt into the river before he reached the other side?' I said sarcastically.

'He wouldn't need to,' she said. 'He must have been standing. He could have crouched down and put out the light, just in case anybody was watching. He'd have to make sure it fitted with his story.'

'You're wrong about Joseph,' I said. 'I've known him for years. He'd not do a thing like this. And I can prove it.'

Rib waited.

'If he *did* get into this costume on the nights he says he saw The Lady, how did he get back over the river to tell us? The boat is still here. We know he couldn't get far by bike. He's not fit enough and I know his tyres are in shreds. Besides, we both saw him running up Lady Lane the first time.'

'There was no burglary the first time,' said Rib. 'He must have made that one up to put people off the scent.'

I was about to continue the argument, but Rib motioned me to be quiet. She stood still, listening intently like a startled deer.

'Someone's coming,' she whispered. 'Get everything back as it was.'

As we bundled the costumes away and pushed the boat under the doors we heard the screech of bicycle brakes.

'Quick,' said Rib. 'We can't go back the way we came. We'll have to work our way back through the allotments and hope nobody sees us.'

We got out on to the lane near our cycles.

'We should be all right if we keep our heads down,' said Rib.

We stopped for a moment to look back down the lane towards the river. A shiny new bike with a big front basket was propped against the fence, and up on the dyke, staring over towards Skelland, was the unmistakable figure of Joseph Jenkins.

'I'm sorry,' said Rib.

Chapter Seventeen

It was Monday. Rib and I sat on some steps at the far end of the school field and waited for Jason. I was feeling very low. I'd had another letter from Emma. Life sounded so ordinary for her, so safe. I had thought life would be dull without her, but now I prayed for it to be ordinary. Every time I thought of Joseph I wanted to cry. Why couldn't everything have stayed the same?

'Want a hanky?' said Rib.

'No thanks,' I said.

'I'm really sorry about Joseph,' she said.

'So am I,' I said.

Tears began to stream down my face. I couldn't stop them. And then the sobs came, great heaving sobs. Rib put her skinny arm round my shoulders.

'Have a good cry,' she said. 'It'll make you feel better.'

'Not it *won't*,' I sobbed. 'I've lost a... friend. He used to make me tea in his silly tea pots... and give me eggs... and d'you know what?'

'Tell me,' she said gently.

'They were usually rotten.'

I laughed and cried at the same time.

'That's better,' she said, pushing a grubby hanky into my hand. 'Wipe the tears away. Here comes Jason. You'll set him off if you're not careful. He gets really upset when other people cry. You wouldn't think so to look at him, would you?'

'What's the plan then?' said Jason briskly. 'When are we going to catch him? I can't stop for long. I'm on third sitting.'

'Don't you think we ought to go to the police?' I said. The words made my throat ache.

'What would we tell them?' said Jason. 'That you've found a boat with two Fancy Dress costumes in it?'

'We'll have to catch him at it,' said Rib. 'Sorry, Sam. It's the only way.'

'What if he doesn't do it again? He may have gone to Thorncoates to destroy the evidence.'

'I reckon he'll try it again before the pipes are covered,' said Jason. 'Can you persuade that Podd creature to let you know when it happens?'

'I think I've seen to that,' said Rib.

'How did you manage it this time?' said Jason admiringly.

'I told her that two burglaries proved nothing,' said Rib. 'I said there was nothing worth having in those houses and that they probably painted little red boxes and stuck them on their houses to make it look as if they needed burglar alarms. She was livid. She said, "You can expect another phone call, Goddard. I shall tell aunty to ring the moment she sees the police car." I said I was so sure there would be no call that I was prepared to wager my bike on it. I told her I'd had a new one last birthday, with posh gears.'

'You wouldn't give it to her, would you?' I said.

'Of course not,' said Rib. 'I'll give her my old one . . . if she can find the tip Dad took it to. I'll even let her borrow my new bicycle pump to blow up the tyres, that is if they haven't got holes in them.'

'We could always put a few holes in them if necessary,' said Jason.

'Stop it!' I said. 'You are treating this as a joke. I hate you!'

'Sorry,' said Jason.

He looked a bit shocked. I was glad.

'If things go the same way as before and something is stolen in the day,' said Rib. 'We can expect Joseph to cross the river that night. He must cycle round to Thorncoates, on his new bike, and wait until dark to bring the boat across.'

'It's very cunning of him to take it over the river,' said Jason. 'The police will never pin it on him if they can't find any evidence in his cottage. Do you think he's buried it on one of those allotments?'

'I hope not,' said Rib. 'They'll never find it in those weeds.'

'We'll have to sneak out,' said Jason.

'I'll ring Sam if I hear from Isabelle,' said Rib. 'And we can decide where to meet.'

'I'm not sneaking out,' I said.

'You'll have to think of an excuse then,' said Rib. 'Tell them you're going on a nature ramble or something.'

'Don't be ridiculous,' I said. 'That wouldn't convince anybody. I suppose I'll *have* to sneak out. It's better than lying. I hate lying.'

The whistle went for third sitting. Jason stood.

'I keep wondering if we should tell someone about all this,' I said. 'It could be dangerous.'

'I know what you mean,' said Jason. 'I think we should agree to tell the police if things seem to be getting out of hand.'

We watched Jason walking up the busy field towards the school.

'That's settled then,' said Rib.

Chapter Eighteen

The phone call came that evening.

'It's me,' said Rib. 'The Carpenters' place has been burgled. Mrs Carpenter's pearls have gone missing. Meet us in the car park. Bring a torch... and don't forget your wellies. It'll be muddy.'

By the time we reached the end of the pipes, the moon was up. Its reflection gleamed up at us from the bottom of the water-filled trench.

'Let's hide behind that digger,' said Rib. 'We should be able to see across to the end of the pipes and Joseph's cottage without being seen ourselves.'

'I hope poor Barker isn't in the pipes,' I said.

'He may have some way of getting out without the workmen spotting him,' said Jason. 'In which case Joseph may have the stuff already.'

'Or we could be wrong,' I said. 'About the pipes and everything.'

We squelched around the huge piece of machinery, holding on to the cold metal to guide ourselves. And then we waited.

We heard the footsteps first. They were slow, very slow, but there was another noise. It was nearer . . . a panting sound came from the other side of the digger . . . It was Barker. He slithered round and snuffled his wet nose up to my face.

The footsteps continued. Someone was on the other side of the digger. A familiar figure was silhouetted against the moonlit sky. Joseph. He strode round the digger and found us there, three crouching spies in the mud.

'What in heaven's name are *you* doing here?' he said, shining a torch at each startled face in turn.

'Joseph,' I said. 'We know everything, about the thefts and the costumes in the boat. We *saw* you in Thorncoates. Why did you do it?'

'Yes,' said Jason. 'You've got some explaining to do.'

'Shall I go for the police?' said Rib.

'Don't do that, lass,' said Joseph. 'I'm not the culprit.'

'Don't believe him,' said Jason. 'Why else would he be skulking about near the pipes?'

'Hear me out,' said Joseph.

'Give him a chance,' I said. 'Let's hear what he's got to say.'

'All right,' said Jason. 'But it had better be good.'

'Yes,' said Rib. 'We know what we saw, don't we, Sam?'

'You're right about some things,' said Joseph. 'I *was* in Thorncoates. I'd been thinking very hard about The Lady and her Fox, and several things didn't add up. Something happened outside my cottage last Monday night. Barker sensed it and barked at the window. I feared the worst and didn't dare look out. The same happened on Wednesday, only that time I did look out. It was drizzling but I saw The Lady and her Fox and it nearly scared the life out of me. I ran to the pub and told Mr Goddard. He got Den Critchley over, but it was only after Den had driven me home that it struck me.'

'Go on. Surprise us,' said Rib sarcastically.

'Barker wasn't afraid,' said Joseph. 'That's what struck me. And if he wasn't, there was no reason why I should be. I went out to the dyke and climbed up to the spot where The Lady had walked down. Barker knew where to go. He was there before me.'

'You don't expect us to believe this tripe do you?' said Jason.

'Don't tell us you met The Lady,' said Rib. 'We're not that stupid.'

'What I saw,' said Joseph, 'were footprints and other marks on the mud. Barker found them, though the rain had nearly washed them away. And he stood there, barking and wagging his tail, as if he could smell a friend.'

'So?' said Rib.

'It was no ghost that had made those tracks,' he said.

'We know *that*,' said Jason. 'We saw them too. Someone used The Fox and Lady story as a cover.'

'And we think it was you,' said Rib. 'The so-called ghost was there on Monday and Wednesday, the evenings after the Holme Burton thefts.'

'And once before Foxing Day,' said Jason. 'Was that a practice run?'

'That I don't know,' said Joseph, 'but I thought that if The Fox and Lady I'd seen were real enough to leave prints, then so was their boat. I borrowed Angela Mycroft's bike and pedalled over to Thorncoates. You seem to know what I found there.'

'That explains everything,' I said. 'Of course it wasn't Joseph. I knew it. He's here for the same reason as us...'

'What rubbish,' said Rib.

'Keep down all of you!' said Jason, peering intently over the digger. 'I think there's someone on the dyke.'

Joseph crouched down beside us with Barker by his side.

'He's near your cottage now,' said Jason.

'I left the radio on in my hobby room,' said Joseph. 'So it would sound as if I were at home. I should keep well down now, lad. We can see the pipes from here. That's what counts.'

We kept still and silent. My knees ached from crouching and my heart pounded with anticipation, but now Joseph was with us I wasn't afraid.

Soon we heard footsteps squelching across the field. A figure stopped at the end of the pipes. We could see her silhouette clearly. It was Nora Hambly. She took a whistle from a large holdall and raised it to her lips. She blew hard, and the signal was answered with a distant bark. I felt Barker's body tense beside me.

Nora waited. We all waited. And eventually Spot emerged from the pipes with a little yelp of relief. There was something round his poor neck, a pouch of some sort.

'Good,' said Nora, removing the pouch.

Then things started to go very wrong. First Spot barked. He knew we were there. Then Barker

128

answered him, running round the digger and slithering happily over to his friends.

'Not you,' hissed Nora.

Her voice sounded different. Hard.

'Go away you stupid animal. What is that fool Joseph doing letting you out at this time of night . . . or perhaps he's with you . . . perhaps he's not so stupid as we thought.'

She picked Barker up and pushed him roughly into the holdall. We heard the zip closing.

This puzzled Spot, who ran around the bag, barking excitedly.

'Shut up Spot,' said Nora, giving him a sharp slap on his back.

She picked up the holdall and turned in our direction. For an awful moment we thought she could see us.

'This bag is so heavy I might just drop it into the river,' she said.

This was more than Joseph could bear.

He stood and squelched round the digger.

'I thought that would get you out of hiding,' said Nora with satisfaction. 'Keep your distance Jenkins.'

She reached in her pocket. Something gleamed. A knife.

'Nora,' said Joseph. 'Not you?'

'Yes, it's me,' she said smugly.

'You don't have to go through with this,' said Joseph. 'Give it up Nora.'

'Not me,' said Nora. 'My Sid was forced to give up. You all made him give up. You threw him off your wretched committee, didn't you? I've never seen him so low. You put that idiot Angela in his place . . . played right into our hands didn't she, her and her vivid imagination? It's been good to see you frightened. It was what you deserved for rejecting my Sid. You,

Critchley and Carpenter ... I made you all squirm. Even Critchley. He thinks he's so efficient. He left his precious keys where anyone could find them. I left my job with him as a protest, but not before I'd had the shed key copied. I replaced it before he could miss it, the idiot. My cleaning jobs have been quite handy one way and another.'

'So *you* tampered with the box?'

'Sid did it the night before the Goddards took over. Then we waited for a nice misty night for me to try out my ghostly Lady act. I only wish I could have been at the pub to see your face that night. I persuaded Sid to go. I knew that was where you'd run to. He was worried that I might not get the boat over the dyke by myself, but I wanted to know that my little trick had convinced you.'

'You got what you wanted,' said Joseph. 'You scared the wits out of me. But why didn't you stop there? Why steal?'

'It was too good an opportunity to miss,' she said. 'And besides, there were still the Carpenters to be dealt with.'

She laughed. It was a mean laugh.

'Please Nora,' said Joseph, stepping forward. 'You know we meant Sid no harm...'

'Don't come any closer,' she said. 'One move and Barker feels this blade. The same if you try to get help. You thought your dog was *so* clever didn't you? My Spot outsmarted the lot of you.'

'So he did,' said Joseph.

He was playing for time. Jason turned to Rib and me.

'I'll get help,' he mouthed.

We nodded, our hearts pounding as he crawled away. There was plenty of cover behind bricks and machinery, but the dogs might give him away.

'How did he do it?' asked Joseph, talking loudly as if he guessed what was happening.

'My Sid trained him. Got him further along the pipes each day until we were ready to use him.'

'Wasn't he seen?'

Nora laughed gleefully.

'No, he stayed in the van, as quiet as a little lamb until Sid was closing up the enclosure. He trained him then, after all the others had gone. Clever, isn't it? It was so easy. Nobody ever suspected ordinary Nora and Sid of taking the jewels, did they?

'I got the brooch when Mrs Carpenter's neighbour came in. She left her keys on the kitchen counter and went into the lounge to chat. As far as they knew I was brewing the tea, but there was plenty of time to nip round to her house and get the brooch. The silly woman had already told us exactly where it was and what she was planning to wear that night. They have a gap in the hedge behind their garages that they use when they visit each other, so I knew I could get in and out without being seen.'

'Didn't Mrs Carpenter and her friend suspect you?' said Joseph.

'No, they may have pots of money, but they haven't a brain cell between them. You'd have laughed to see me running after her when she left saying, "I think you've forgotten your keys." It was simple to pass the brooch over to Sid when I went over to tell him what time to pick me up that night. Spot was down the pipes before the police arrived.'

'What about the ring?'

'Simple,' she said. 'Sid was up his ladder checking some gutters. The bathroom window was open. He picked the ring off the side of the basin on his way down. When he got back over to the site he popped Spot down the pipes. He'd trained him to go down far enough so he wouldn't be seen. The other men were in the hut having their lunch at the time. He went to join them and sent a couple of the lads over to clean the gutters. It couldn't have been easier. The police spoke to him, of course, but their job wasn't made any easier by the fact that the woman wasn't sure where she'd taken off her ring. People like that don't deserve to keep their jewels.'

'Don't you think they'll be on to you this time?'

'Sid thought that. He wanted to leave it there, but I'd not forgotten Carpenter. It was just a question of waiting for the right moment. Serves him right for leaving a string of pearls lying about. She asked him to take them into Cumbermouth to have the clasp mended and the idiot left them on the hall table. Luckily I spotted them before she did. I bet she's furious with him. I took them over to Sid in a medicine box this afternoon. I told Mrs Carpenter it was something for his bad chest and that he'd forgotten to take a dose this morning. It was a pity to do it to her in a way ... but they can afford it ... And now Sid and I will have a bit of money to make a fresh start. We've no intention of staying where we're not wanted.'

'The story about seeing a fox...?'

'All lies,' she said. 'Good at acting, aren't we? Even the bungalow was a lie. We live there all right, but we only rent the place. We've got somewhere much nicer than that, been saving for it for years. After what's happened to Sid, we're going as far away as possible ... and we won't be sending you our change of address.'

She pushed the pouch into her pocket.

'And don't think I don't know you are playing for time, Mr Jenkins. It won't do you any good. There is nobody else about. By the time you got help we'd be

132

long gone, and who's going to believe an old man who thinks he sees ghosts? Besides, I wanted you to know. It makes it all the more satisfying.'

She picked up the bag and began to walk away over the mud. Spot followed obediently.

'Come along,' she said to Joseph. 'But keep your distance.'

Joseph stood his ground.

'I know you'll come,' she called without turning. There was menace in her voice.

Joseph did not move.

'You wouldn't want Barker to slip into the river, would you?' She turned. 'Don't think I wouldn't dare,' she said. 'If you come along like a good chap you can watch me do my Fox and Lady act and Barker might get safely over the river. It's got to look right in case anybody else happens to be watching. You will be so frightened by the ghost that you'll rush off to the pub to tell your cronies ... Only about the ghost, though, or I can promise you'll not see Barker again.'

Joseph followed her. We waited as the footsteps retreated.

'Let's hope Jason has got on to the Thorncoates police,' whispered Rib, once they were out of earshot. 'I was terrified she'd hear him.'

When she reached the lane, Nora crouched behind the hedge. She took the cloak and hood from her bag, zipping it up again to trap Barker.

'Why doesn't Joseph grab Barker?' said Rib.

'Because Nora's mad,' I said. 'And she's still got the knife.'

Nora put on the cloak and bent down to fit the fox costume on Spot.

'Now's his chance,' said Rib. 'What's he playing at? Is he in league with her?'

'Don't be stupid,' I said. 'He knows we'll get help.

Why risk getting hurt? There's no telling what she might do if he takes her on.'

Nora held the holdall inside her cloak and walked down Lady Lane towards the dyke. Spot walked meekly at her side and Joseph followed at a safe distance.

'Do you think she does weight training on the quiet?' said Rib. 'I'm sure I couldn't carry Barker very far.'

As Nora passed Joseph's cottage, clouds covered the moon and it became hard to see her.

'Come on,' said Rib. 'It's all right to follow them now.'

By the time we reached Joseph's cottage, Nora had gone over the dyke. Joseph crouched helplessly at the bottom of the dyke, unable to see if Barker was safe or not. We crept up beside him. He nodded grimly. I squeezed his arm. It wasn't safe to talk. On the other side of the dyke the boat set off. We could hear the chug-chug of the motor. We worked our way up the dyke on our stomachs. None of us cared about the mud any more. We lay at the top, hidden by grass and thistle, and watched.

Nora was half way across. The lamp lay in the bottom of the boat and made her cloak gleam. When she was half way across she seemed to disappear. The lamp was out, but we could hear the boat chugging until she reached the other side. By straining our eyes, we could see Nora clambering up the bank to Sid.

They were still dragging the boat over the top of the dyke when the police cars arrived. Nora and Sid made no attempt to escape. They waited on the dyke with Spot and the holdall beside them, posing in the glare of the police car headlights, like actors in a pantomime. We stood. There was no point in hiding any more.

It was only as the police approached that Nora moved. The moon came out for a second and she looked back across the river to see us standing there. Before the officers could stop her she snatched up the holdall, ran down the dyke towards the river and hurled it into the water.

'That's for you, Joseph Jenkins,' she shouted, her voice carrying clearly across the water. 'I hope you're satisfied.'

Joseph groaned. We watched in horror as the holdall sank beneath the water.

'Oh, no,' said Rib. 'Let's get him out.'

She began to kick off her wellies and would have leapt straight in if I hadn't stopped her.

'Don't be silly,' I said. 'You'll drown.'

'I'll get him,' said Joseph, throwing off his jacket and boots.

On the opposite bank, Nora was being held by two policemen. Sid and Spot stood meekly beside them.

'Thought your dog was good at tricks, did you, Jenkins?' she cried. 'Let's see him get out of that!'

'Stay where you are, sir,' called one of the officers.

'There's no telling where it is,' I said. 'The current may have taken it anywhere.'

'It's too late, sir,' called the officer.

'He's right,' said Rib, putting her thin arm around him. 'Sorry, Joseph.'

We were still standing on the dyke when Jason arrived.

'Did they get her?' he said breathlessly.

'Yes,' said Rib. 'And Sid.'

'That's great,' said Jason. 'The police will want statements from us. The officer I spoke to said they were very keen to talk to Nora and Sid about the latest theft. It was beginning to be too much of a coincidence that one or other of them had been around when anything went missing, and nobody had seen either of them since they left work this afternoon. We'd better get back to The Fox and Lady. I didn't stop to explain to Mum and Dad. They must be missing us by now.'

He looked from one sad face to another, puzzled.

'What's up with you lot?' he said. 'We did it, proved there was no ghost and caught Nora Hambly in the act.'

'It's Barker,' I said.

'Did she take him over the river?' he said. 'The police will soon return him.'

'They'll not do that,' said Joseph quietly.

'Nora drowned him,' said Rib. 'She threw the holdall in the river.'

'I'm sorry, Joseph,' said Jason. 'I thought she was bluffing.'

'You weren't to know, lad,' said Joseph.

His voice wobbled.

'Barker's gone,' he said. 'But it was in a good cause. At least we can all feel safe again.'

The clouds released the moon and from along the dyke came a sound that made us turn. A small animal hurtled along the dyke towards us, barking urgently. It reached us and flung its muddy body into Joseph's arms.

'Well·I'll be blowed,' said Joseph. 'It's my Barker. He got out.'

'That's amazing,' said Jason.

'Brilliant,' I said.

'Aye,' said Joseph. 'He's a regular little Houdini.'

'Unless he had help,' said Rib.

There was a strange expression on her face, not of fear, more of wonder. We followed her gaze and saw that, at the place where we had first seen Barker, a translucent figure stood. She was cloaked in white and seemed to turn her hooded head in our direction before picking up the animal at her side. As she moved down towards the water we felt no fear. Barker stood erect, and we watched in silence as she glided across the river towards Thorncoates. We held our breath as she climbed effortlessly up the opposite bank. And after she had gently placed her fox on the grass, we thought she looked back towards us for a second, before she and the fox faded from view.

'The curse is broken,' said Joseph. 'Our lack of fear has freed The Lady and The Fox of Skelland.'

SLI